Being Human

Andrew R Bedlington

A CIP catalogue record for this book is available from the British Library

ISBN 978-1-7399983-2-5

Edited by Judy Brulo and Eleanor Baggaley
Typeset & cover design by
Eleanor Baggaley, Snowdrop Publishing
First Published 2023 by Rob Cole

For Pat
a belated thriller

This novel is a work of fiction. Names and characters are the product of the author's imagination. Any resemblance to persons, living or dead, is entirely coincidental.

Acknowledgements

Special thanks to Judy Brulo, so much more than an editor extraordinaire. Offering her extensive knowledge and guidance, she helped me to get the book to where it is today.

And to the ex-Superintendent Richard Agar for his invaluable police-related advice that helped to ensure authenticity.

Preface

Over recent years, I have produced various examples of written prose, with some success. These have usually been in the form of technical comments to trade magazines about my occupation as a plumber. Others have taken the form of letters to local newspapers where the likes of Angry from Atherstone regularly rant. I like to think my offerings are essentially more entertaining than that. Pat repeatedly told me they were; asking, 'Why haven't you written a book of your own?'

'Okay, Pat, I will.'

I knew she was a prolific reader, preferring a something-to-get-your-teeth-stuck-into thriller.

'Pat, I'll write you a thriller.'

Tragically, Pat passed away at the end of 2021. Her son, William, my son-in-law, reminded me how his mum looked forward to reading my stuff. For my part, I expressed my regret for not producing that thriller in time for her to read it. I put it to William: did he think it a good idea for me to attempt to produce a belated thriller—my first book—as a tribute to Pat?

He readily agreed.

Part One

Chapter 1

A Jack Russell's Story

Spot's first memory. Ah! It was as if it had happened yesterday. He lived with his parents and was the only remaining puppy in the litter. His owners called him Spot, inevitable really, on account of the big black spot on his white coat. Life was good. Those long walks on the beach, running for miles and miles. It was idyllic. Then, things changed.

One summer morning, towards noon, a car pulled up in the drive. An immaculately attired guy stepped out. He opened the passenger door for his partner, also dressed to the nines. As they were shown into the house, they made a point of wiping their feet and voicing their please and thank yous exaggeratedly.

Over coffee, in proper cups and saucers, Spot listened in on the humans' conversation. Shock, horror! His owners had decided to emigrate. They would take Spot's parents with them, but they would sell him off—separate him from his family. His fate would be with this weird couple. The deal was done. His owners were taken in and Spot ... powerless.

The next thing the Jack Russell knew, he was scooped up and dumped onto the back seat of his new owners' car on top of numerous copies of The Sun. They had obviously expected their acquisition might not be in full control of his bowel movements.

Spot's sensitive little nose immediately detected an earthy, woody smell—cannabis.

Things got worse. The bloke was a terrible driver. After hours of being thrown around all over the place and Spot throwing up everywhere—the newspapers now impossible to read—a synthetic voice announced, 'You have reached your destination.' Spot felt a mix of relief that the car had stopped, and fear of what the future would hold.

As night closed in, streetlights flickered on, to reveal the grim back streets of an inner-city and a rundown terraced slum, more than in need of TLC. Dodgy-looking characters abounded. Spot would soon learn that this wretched array of flotsam and jetsam would be sidling up to the Wasters' ground-floor window to satiate their drug habit.

The 'lady' opened the rear door of the car and, picking Spot up roughly, carried him to the backyard. She unceremoniously dumped him with a stern warning, 'Be a good boy, or else!'

Thanks for nothing, Spot thought.

Cowering in the shadowy recesses of the yard were other sad-looking dogs. They snarled a greeting. *This doesn't look good,* Spot figured. *Hmm . . . need to make myself scarce.*

As he retreated to a spare corner of the yard, the sudden metallic sound of the gate latch diverted his attention. Instinctively, he cowered, ears down, panting, wondering what fate awaited him next.

The gate squeaked open. A slight, hunched, head-scarved figure stepped in, turned, closed the gate, furtively scanned the yard and click-clacked her way towards the kitchen door. The resident dogs didn't react—their noses accustomed to her cheap perfume, *L'Odeur de la Nuit*, mixed with weed.

Phew! Just the girl next door requesting a favour.

The nerve-racked Jack Russell allowed himself to relax, just a little. But then, only a few minutes later, an equally suspicious high-heeled being appeared. Spot finally realised: *Oh my God! Not just drugs— this place is doubling up as a knocking shop!*

'Hey, you. Newbie.' snapped a stocky-looking, wide-jawed crossbreed, coming out of the shadows. 'Judging from the black spot on your white coat, I guess you're Spot. Ha-ha! Come over here, Spot and I'll give you the low-down.'

Butch briefed Spot on his role in the household. Sir and Madam kept the dogs there to deter intruders.

'You see, Newbie, Sir and Madam are shady dealers. We get all sorts sniffing around this joint. You do your job, and they'll treat you right—more or less.'

If that was meant to cheer Spot up, it missed the target. This feeling of utter misery was nothing he'd experienced before in his short life. The little Jack Russell lifted his head and howled for his parents, brothers and sisters.

Someone shouted from the suspiciously lit bedroom window, 'Shut that bloody racket!' This was accompanied by a beer bottle smashing into the yard, narrowly missing Spot. *It couldn't get much worse, surely?* Spot hoped as he slunk into the leaky kennel. And amazingly, despite the hunger pangs, he eventually drifted off to sleep.

Spot's new owners had to return the hire car the next day. Sir wasn't happy about that. And the posh clothes, which she was extremely reluctant to send back. There were high-pitched screams and a Niagara Falls-worth of tears when Sir yelled, 'Look 'ere, Marlene! *I'm* ditching the Rolls, so *you* have to part with your exquisite rags. Come on. We have to get on with stuff. We can't be out of action for too long, or our deals will go sour. Our customers need satisfaction, or you'll not have even a stitch to your name.'

That seemed to convince her. The screaming stopped.

After a few more intolerable weeks, Spot decided he'd had enough. Though those weeks were not entirely unprofitable and had afforded him some useful information. Sir, aka the Waster, would return frequently from who-knows-where and at who-knows-when o'clock, but always in a drunken stupor. He would lurch through the back gate of the yard. Spot would hear his fumbled attempts at unlocking, slamming shut, and relocking the gate before he staggered noisily through the kitchen door.

Spot waited for his moment.

The next Saturday night, Sir, as usual, (especially on a Saturday night) wobbled in through the gate, tripping over one of the other unfortunate dogs who happened to be out for a pee. The language was industrial. In the commotion, Sir forced himself to his feet and threw himself into the house, completely forgetting to close the gate. Miracle! This was Spot's chance for freedom. A no-brainer. Out he shot, running for his life, not even looking back to see if the other dogs had followed.

After a couple of miles, Spot's strength was failing. Those weeks with Sir and Madam had left him in poor health. He had to rest. He reached a slip road. There was a hedge on the other side.

That will have to do, he thought. *I can't go on any longer.* Near to exhaustion, Spot used his last remaining strength to race across the slip road to safety. In his desperation, he didn't notice the headlights. The car had nowhere to go and caught Spot's hind leg. Thwack! He squealed but managed to drag himself to the verge, yelping in agony.

The car screeched to a halt. The occupants, a man and a lady jumped out.

'Oh, my God, Ronan! We've just run over a dog. I think he's alive, but look at his hind leg, it's a mess!'

'Quick, Shannon, we need to pick him up, if he'll let us, and take him to a vet.' Spot hadn't the strength or inclination to resist. Anything would be better than going back to Sir and Madam Waster.

They sped off with the man driving like Lewis Hamilton and the lady cradling Spot in her arms on the back seat. Suddenly, the lady and Spot were thrown forward as the man braked violently, narrowly avoiding a bus that had pulled out without indicating. The lady yelled, and Spot whined.

'Hey, Ronan! We need to get home in one piece.'

'Give me a break, Love, I'm trying my best. It's a bit of a contrast to our quiet day in the Malverns. My brain needs time to recalibrate. Ring the vet's out-of-hours service. See if they can see the dog. We should be there in twenty minutes.'

Ronan and Shannon arrived at the vet's surgery. The vet scanned the dog for a microchip—nada. They had no idea who he belonged to. After examining Spot's leg, the vet's initial diagnosis was that it was fractured. He would need to stabilise him overnight, make him comfortable and X-ray it in the morning to assess the damage accurately.

Ronan and Shannon agreed to foot the bill and take ownership of the injured stray. At least they had hearts, unlike Sir and Madam Waster.

'Let's call him Spot,' Shannon said.

Chapter 2

A Surprise in the Malverns for Spot

Ronan and Shannon were enjoying a cup of tea and warm mince pies in their heated, cosy new conservatory. It was one of those bitter days in November, the early morning autumnal mist clearing to reveal a bright azure sky.

'This is a perfect day for a trip to the Malverns with Spot. What say you, Shannon?'

'Absolutely, Ronan. Let's do it.'

Ronan fitted the newly purchased, padded load liner into their 4x4. With the rear seats down, this provided a wealth of room for Spot and the paraphernalia. They set off, anticipating one of the best days out. Spot felt the excitement.

The air suspension of the Macan Turbo afforded a luxurious super-smooth ride. So smooth that Spot dozed off almost instantly, waking only when they turned onto the steep gradient of the gravel car park at their destination. The sun beamed down on the small party as they trekked up the rough path to the top of the Herefordshire Beacon. Surprisingly, there were only a handful of walkers around. Ronan, a tad short of breath, and feeling Spot's energy, let him off his lead.

Shannon suggested walking the ridge between the peaks. She thought it would be relatively easy-going. Thankfully, by the time they reached the next peak, Spot had slowed down from 100 mph to a more normal pace. So, Ronan and Shannon felt they could relax a bit and enjoy the day.

At that moment, Spot disappeared into the gorse bushes as fast as his little legs could carry him.

'Oh, my God! Where's Spot?' Shannon asked, running over to where they had last seen him. 'Help me look for him, Ronan, for goodness' sake.'

'Spot? Spot? Come on! Here, boy!' Ronan yelled.

The longer it went on, the more they panicked. It was twenty minutes since he disappeared. They sat on the cold, damp rocks, waiting. Nothing. But just as they thought they'd have to report their loss to the authorities, who should emerge, looking strangely spooked?

‘Where the hell have you been, ol’ fella?’ asked Ronan.

Spot had caught sight of a squirrel. He had to chase after it, of course. He’d followed the scent of the squirrel to another path, where a couple were sitting on a bench having a heated row. The man was gesticulating wildly. The woman looked strange. At Spot’s approach, she froze, turned her head and focussed her steely gaze directly at him. Spot was unable to react, unable to move. Who was she? The beautiful Kayleigh had met Declan Mitchell, a portly, self-employed electrician when she and her husband engaged him to do a substantial amount of work at their house. Over the following weeks, it became apparent that she and Declan had a lot in common. Although they differed on religion—she was an ardent Spiritualist—Declan didn’t believe in anything, really; they both enjoyed reading and even writing, in a recreational sort of way.

Increasingly, the two of them longed for the next meeting, realising that their connection was rapidly escalating.

Despite her marital status, Kayleigh was, if she dared to admit it, a loner, fiercely in charge of her own destiny. Anyone who befriended her needed to discover this as quickly as possible. Failing to recognise her rigid stance had the potential to unleash who knows what.

Her husband had learned this to his peril. It was an uncomfortable match, which she often regretted. But since she'd met Declan, she found herself questioning her previously irrefutable instincts. Not with her husband, but perhaps with Declan she could find the equilibrium her soul had been searching for. With this thought, she relaxed into a long-awaited peace. Kayleigh and her husband, who made a pretence of emotional distress, quickly parted company, and she moved in with Declan. She would find, in due course, that this peace was fragile.

Just as Kaleigh had thrown on Declan's switch when he first met her, now, inexplicably, she'd turned it firmly off. Try as he might, he couldn't put his finger on the direct cause. And despite the soul searching, as far as he was concerned, it was over. *How would he explain this to her?* Maybe a trip to the country, out of the house in a neutral environment, would give him the headspace he needed to broach the subject.

'Hey, Kayleigh! How about a walk in the Malverns?' Declan suggested. 'It's a nippy day, but it's sunny. Should be lovely up there. What d'you say?'

'Sounds great. I love it there,' she replied.

Oblivious of what the day had in store for her, an excited Kayleigh packed a picnic basket. Wedges of cheese, cherry tomatoes and crusty bread, along with a bottle of Australian Chardonnay.

With rucksacks jam-packed, they struggled up a steep, stony path. Exhausted, they slumped onto a bench. The view from the Herefordshire Beacon was magnificent, stretching for miles on this glorious day. It didn't take long for them to unpack and tuck into their lunch.

Declan gathered his thoughts. It was now or never.

He had to tell her.

As his words sank in, Kayleigh felt the urge to lash out at her new enemy. The adage, *hell hath no fury like a woman scorned,* doesn't get near it. Jumping to her feet, scattering the food and wine, she grabbed him by the throat with unbelievable force. 'Repeat what you just said to me, so I'm certain,' she screamed.

Choking and spluttering, he countered, 'For goodness' sake, let go of my throat.'

Kayleigh released her grip. 'Come on, then. Out with it.' Recovering himself, he continued, 'The fact is, Kayleigh, I just can't explain it. The spark's gone. I'm just not in love with you anymore.'

An uncontrollable, primaeval force welled up inside her, engulfing Kayleigh's body and her spiritualist soul completely. To kill Declan would be too easy on him. Instead, she would invade his body so that he would never be free of her. She would make him pay.

A Jack Russell watched, unseen, as Kayleigh vapourised into a shimmering grey ether, first circling, and then seeping into Declan's body. Declan spoke, but it was the woman's thin, piercing voice Spot heard.

'Ha! I'm going to haunt you for forever and a day,' she cackled. 'I shall luxuriate in your punishment for abandoning me.'

Spot turned tail and ran, almost crashing into his owners, who had come in search of him.

'Ronan, the poor dog's spooked.'

'My God!' Ronan exclaimed, looking in the direction from which Spot had come. The shimmering grey shape, noticing the new arrivals, floated away.

Chapter 3

Today

Ronan was late: *that effing dog was probably chasing imaginary rabbits again.* Shannon squinted through the window into the early evening winter gloom. The streetlights were already on, casting ghostly haloes of light around them. Finally, Ronan's familiar shape appeared on the village green. He waved. Shannon opened the door to him, but only Spot, the Jack Russell, looking cowed and spooked, stood on the mat. The light from the hallway fell across the lone dog. He was wet, and yet it hadn't been raining, and was that a drop of red paint on his back?

Shannon felt a shadow passing across her, bringing shivers of dread and unwelcome memories of the apparition in the Malverns.

Spot padded in. She was just about to get him some food when she heard next door's doorbell.

What the . . . ? she thought. In the battle between curiosity and unlikely courage, curiosity won. Forgetting all about Spot, she walked up the two stone porch steps of No. 9 and rang the bell, thinking, *I shouldn't be so nosey.*

The door opened. Her jaw dropped. It was Ronan, who, with a confused air, enquired, 'Can I help you?'

'R-Ronan? It's me . . . your wife. What the hell are you doing here?'

Then, looking over his shoulder, something caught her eye. Through the partially open kitchen door, a figure appeared to be at the sink, hovering above the ground. Long, white hair tumbled down its shimmering grey, diaphanous gown, partially concealing her oh-so-slim body. Shannon thought she saw a flash of light in the sink. *Was it a reflection from the streetlights?*

'What's going on, Ronan?'

'Oh, it's Declan, he's just washing up.' He called across, 'Declan, come and meet the wife.'

The kitchen door fully opened, and a portly chap rolled towards them, beaming from ear to ear. The apparition was nowhere to be seen. Shannon's head was swimming. She crumpled to the floor. Out like a light.

The next day Shannon woke with a humdinger of a headache, but couldn't recall why. Scowling over her coffee, she rubbed her head, 'Ouch. It hurts. How did I manage that, Ronan?'

'Don't you remember? You fainted on Declan's porch last night—probably banged your head,' he suggested.

'Oh, did I? Declan? Huh! I can't remember a thing.'

As they made breakfast, Shannon, still confused, flicked the radio on.

> 'Breaking news!' The radio announcer shouted. 'The bodies of two teenage girls have been found in a Warwickshire canal. Of course, we'll bring you more when we have it.'

They looked at each other, toast in mid-air. 'You walk Spot on a Warwickshire canal,' Shannon said as if cross-questioning a witness.

'Well, there are quite a few canals in Warwickshire, Your Honour,' he countered. Shannon's eyebrows narrowed.

During the rest of the morning, it became clear Spot was not himself. He turned away from his usual left-over scrambled egg and toast, simply taking occasional sips from his water bowl.

'That dog's a pain.' muttered Ronan. Cursing inwardly, he suddenly realised Spot's dip in the rat-infested canal water the day before could have done its worst. Weil's disease.

Somehow, he'd need to get him to the vet without Shannon knowing.

'No, he's not.' Shannon countered, interrupting Ronan's thoughts, 'You just tease him all the time. Spot has a love-hate relationship with you: he loves you taking him for walks and hates you the rest of the time!'

'You can talk, Shannon. You're just as bad.'

The canine, sardonic look that Spot flashed towards his owners, appeared to confirm their conversation. Ronan felt as guilty as hell.

'I wouldn't take him too far today,' Shannon advised. 'He looked like a drowned rat when he turned up on the doorstep last night. Goodness knows why. It hadn't been raining. Why didn't you clean him up when we got back from next door? He stank to high heaven, and apparently, I was in no fit state.'

'Yeah, yeah! I'll make sure to do it if there's a next time, Shannon,' Ronan replied, warning lights flashing. 'Er ...okay, maybe I'll take our other route. It's a bit shorter. They're forecasting a drop in temperature, so I might put his coat on.'

'Good idea.'

'Come on, Spot. Walkies.'

Ronan fetched his thick coat and walking boots out of the under-stairs cupboard. Instead of the excited, wagging tail response, Spot hadn't shifted. 'Hey! Come on, Spot. Time to go.'

Rather gingerly, Spot ambled over to have his lead put on. Ronan felt the dog's nose. It was warm—not a good sign.

'It's a good thing we're only taking the short route, ol' fella,' he said, pulling Spot's dreaded dog coat out of the drawer.

'Maybe you should take him to the vet,' Shannon suggested.

'Er . . . yeah! I'll keep an eye on him. See you later.'

Shannon had forgotten the Bodies-in-the-Canal story. So, when she turned on the radio to listen to Pop Master, she was taken aback to hear the news flash revealing the latest update—and it wasn't good.

> *The pathologist recorded the two girls' deaths as single, but fatal knife wounds to each victim. At this time, the police have no motive to go on. Consequently, they are appealing for anyone who saw anything suspicious to come forward.*
>
> *The bodies were found yesterday evening on the Coventry Canal, at Bridge Fifty, just south of*

Polesworth, Warwickshire. As a popular route for dog walkers, cyclists and schoolkids taking a shortcut, the police surmise somebody may have noticed something.

Shannon turned the radio off. She looked out of the window. Ronan was back from his walk and in the garden busy tidying up the fallen leaves. Spot was with him. She was puzzled. *Why were they back so late yesterday?* Something wasn't quite right. She heard the back door open and automatically put the kettle on.

'How's Spot?' she asked, as Ronan dumped his coat and shoes in the hall.

'Seems to have perked up. Look, he's chomping away at his food, so he must be feeling better.'

Relieved at Spot's recovery, a thankful Ronan settled onto his favourite barstool next to Shannon in the small kitchen. As he took his second sip of tea, his wife repeated the news she'd just heard. Ronan spluttered, choked and quickly replaced his cup on the coaster.

'Are you alright, Ronan?' Shannon asked, watching him struggle to mop up his shirt and trousers.

'Yeah, I'm fine. I pinched one of the last cherry tomatoes. It must have got stuck in my throat.'

Shannon's sceptical frown suggested otherwise.

Ronan swigged what was left of his tea and announced his intention to finish a few jobs before dark, in the greenhouse, which doubled as his man cave. He looked down at his trembling hands, thinking, *I've got to sort myself out somehow, or I'll really go crazy.*

Chapter 4

The Day Before—How Spot Got Wet

It was early afternoon. Shannon was out shopping and there was a knock at the door. 'Oh, hi. I'm sorry to bother you, I'm Declan Mitchell, from No. 9—your new next-door neighbour. I hope you don't mind me asking—I've seen you walking your dog. Would you mind if I tag along now and then? I really need the exercise—been putting on quite a bit of weight lately, and I'm determined to get it off. I thought a few hearty walks would help.'

'Hi, Declan, I'm Ronan. I hope you'll be happy here. It's a nice, quiet street. My wife, Shannon, is out at the moment but I'm sure you'll meet her before too long. The walks; yes, you'd be very welcome to join me. If you want to come along today, I'll be taking Spot out for his afternoon walk in a few minutes.'

The trio took the route onto the canal at Polesworth. Ronan decided Declan seemed an easy-going sort: chatting away as if they'd known each other for years. It was strange: there was something familiar about him.

They left the reaches of town, meeting fewer fellow walkers as they headed along the towpath into the open countryside. They were approaching one of the arched brick canal bridges when two teenage schoolgirls came into view, both glued to their mobile phones. The path was getting narrower and very muddy. As the girls got closer, still with their phones in their faces, the inevitable happened. The fetchingly pretty one walked slap-bang into Declan. She bounced off him in one direction; he rebounded in the other, and Spot ended up in the canal, headfirst. The girl's friend, cursing, helped her up. By good fortune, no one was hurt, but the girl's reaction was notable.

'You fat bastard,' she yelled. 'You could have had me in the canal along with that stupid dog.'

Ronan hauled Spot out with the extendable lead that, thankfully, was still attached. The once pristine dog was now a sorry sight, dripping with dirty, smelly water. Declan's face was a picture—grim—suggesting he would exact revenge whenever possible.

The two girls shot off, shouting out that it would be Ronan and Declan's fault if they were late home.

Ronan, Declan, and Spot continued their walk, with Ronan keeping a concerned eye on Spot. He was mindful of the dangers of Weil's disease, so easily caught in rat-infested canal water. Suddenly, he spotted something lying in the grass. It was a mobile phone which must have been flung out during the encounter. They immediately checked their pockets—they'd both got theirs.

'It must be that stroppy girl's,' Declan said, picking it up and putting it into his pocket.

'If it is, then I expect she'll be calling from another phone when she realises she's dropped it,' Ronan said.

True enough, only minutes later ... Declan answered it, putting it on speaker.

'Is that my phone you've got?' a shrieky voice asked.

'Yes, it is.'

'Are you still on the canal?'

'Yes, by Bridge Fifty, just up from where you bumped into us.'

'I don't believe this. I'm on my way. My parents ain't gonna be 'appy, me being so late. I'm in enough trouble as it is.' That was it. She hung up.

Declan turned to Ronan with a shrug. 'Obnoxious, or what?'

While Ronan was relieving himself behind the hedge, Declan yelled, 'Hey, Ronan! You might be surprised when you get back. Don't panic.'

Ronan wondered what the hell he was going on about. But when he emerged from the bushes, Declan was nowhere to be seen. Instead—there stood an extremely attractive woman dressed in shimmering grey.

The woman smiled an instantly disarming smile, declaring, 'Declan has gone away for a while, and I shall be temporarily replacing him. You can call me Kayleigh.' Ronan was magnetised. Somehow, he felt he knew her, and as if in a trance, he thought he might be falling in love, literally, at first sight.

The squelch of approaching feet jolted him out of his gooey stupor. Finally, the nasty bit of work appeared, arm in arm with her friend.

'Where's that fat bastard with my phone?' Miss Nasty spat out.

With both girls' backs to the water, Kayleigh moved within inches of the bolshy girl's face, fixing her with an icy stare. Miss Nasty pulled her friend closer.

Kayleigh's evil energy erupted. 'Is this what you're looking for?' she asked, handing the schoolgirl her phone.

Ronan was wondering how the woman had got hold of it when Miss Nasty snatched it away. As she did so, the sparkle of the girl's surprisingly elegant necklace caught Ronan's eye. It took only a split second for Kayleigh to one-handedly yank it off her, while with the other, she whipped out a shiny dagger, slashing that pretty neck from ear to ear. The next slash cut the other girl's scream short!

While the life drained from them, Kayleigh shoved the vile creature and her friend into the canal, where the unforgiving waters slowly swallowed their lifeless bodies.

It was all Ronan could do to stop himself from throwing up. What the hell had just happened? He tried to ask but found himself unable to speak. And then, when Kayleigh suggested she and Ronan should depart the scene immediately, he was content to go along with her.

After a while, she produced the necklace. 'You keep that safe,' she ordered, handing it over.

It was getting dark, so Ronan decided it would be expedient to find the shortest route back. As they walked and talked, he began to feel a tangible bond with Kayleigh. And despite the desperate circumstances, he had no desire for the walk to end.

'I'm sorry, Ronan, it has to, for now,' Kayleigh replied to Ronan's unspoken sentiment.

And with that, right in front of his eyes, the beautiful creature gradually morphed back into the roly-poly form that was Declan Mitchell.

Ronan was still in shock when they approached the village—fortunately, having seen very few people on the way.

They were crossing the village green towards his house when the sight of Shannon silhouetted against the lights of the lounge window made him hesitate. He waved. She waved back. He needed to think quickly. So, leaving stinking Spot on his doorstep, he scooted next door with Declan, hoping, that when Shannon opened the door, she wouldn't notice the mess the dog was in.

Chapter 5

Two Days After Spot Got Wet

The next morning, Declan was waiting outside to join Ronan and Spot. Struggling to appear in control, Ronan greeted his neighbour with, 'Hi, Declan. You're keen. Maybe we can go a different way today.'

'Yeah, of course.'

Ronan didn't want to make any reference regarding the events of two days ago. His head just couldn't handle it.

They arrived at the canal, turning left instead of right. The mist seemed reluctant to lift. As soon as the town was behind them Ronan relieved Spot of his coat and released his lead. Rather than shooting off like an arrow in search of all those smells that keep dogs occupied, he merely stood there.

'Perhaps he doesn't like my company,' Declan said with a chuckle.

Finally, Ronan coaxed Spot into moving—albeit at a much slower pace and keeping his distance from Declan.

'I can see why you call him Spot,' observed Declan.

'Yeah,' Ronan said as he looked at the big black spot in the middle of his contrasting snowy white coat.

Drat! Ronan thought, horrified to see that the red blood spot was still evident. I'll have to wait for my chance to rub it off when Declan isn't watching.

Just then, a distant buffeting reached their ears. From behind them, a helicopter shifted into view. The noise, increasing and now almost bursting their eardrums.

'Quick! Under the trees.' Ronan shouted, sweeping Spot into his arms. There, they cowered until the din of the black and yellow aircraft swung away.

'Blimey, that's a police helicopter!' Ronan yelled as they both stared at each other, fearful of the potential outcome.

The helicopter incident prompted Ronan to ask, 'Declan, I've been wondering: how much do you remember about yesterday?'

'Well, we went for a pleasant walk and then went home. Why do you ask?'

'Uh, no reason.'

Ronan, mind completely at sixes and sevens, kicked on the pace while trying to keep the conversation to a minimum. They were back at Declan's in no time.

'Cuppa tea?' Declan offered.

Ronan thanked him but declined; instead, he hurried back to No. 11 with Spot. Shannon wasn't at home. She returned while he was making a coffee.

'Hi, Love,' she said. 'I've been to the GP. Wanted him to check that bang on my head I had yesterday—just in case. The skin's broken and I'll have a massive bruise, but there's no harm done. Hey, Ronan! Are you listening?' Ronan sat down on his favourite barstool, and with a heavy sigh, announced, 'I can't do this anymore.'

Mystified by his unexpected remark, 'Can't do what anymore?' Shannon asked.

He stared into his wife's fearful eyes, cupped her hands in his, sucked in a deep breath and confessed every detail: the paranormal, weird Declan-Kayleigh switch, his hypnotic attraction to Kayleigh. The brutal murder of the schoolgirls, Spot ending up in the canal ... everything. That done, he broke down, signalling his intention to go to the police.

Simply not capable of taking it all in, a trembling Shannon, tears cascading down her face, stumbled her way across the kitchen. Hands shaking, she tried to make a cup of tea, desperately trying to cling on to some sort of normality.

The doorbell rang.

Shannon jumped. ‘Oh, m-my G-God. Who can that be?’ she stammered.

Ronan didn’t look up. Giving him daggers, she teetered to the door. It was Declan, wearing his trademark smile. ‘Hi! I’ve run out of milk, Shannon. I couldn’t trouble you for a drop, could I? Oh, my! Are you okay?’

Incensed, Shannon slammed the door shut, but it was instantly thrown back open as Kayleigh floated in.

Shannon staggered back, but Kayleigh closed in on her, grabbing her neck. Ronan’s knee-jerk reaction to protect his wife sent the barstool crashing to the floor. ‘Back off, Ronan! I know your intention, but I can’t allow you to go through with it,’ Kayleigh screeched.

Kayleigh knew Ronan would spill the beans. She had to act. In a flash, she pulled out the silver dagger. Ronan was rooted to the spot. He knew what was coming! With a heinous cackle, showing not one ounce of mercy, Kayleigh slit Shannon’s throat and then Ronan’s. One by one, slash, slash! Their bodies crumpled to the ground, blood spurting from their throats.

Spot hid on his bed, trembling, trying to make himself invisible. Would he be Kayleigh's next victim?

Observing her handiwork with a smirk of pride, Kayleigh calmly rinsed the murder weapon under the kitchen tap, dried her hands, went over to the house telephone, picked up the receiver with the towel still in her hand, and dialled 999.

Spot saw it all.

Meanwhile: Declan

Declan was relaxing, watching daytime TV, when he heard sirens. His body tensed. *Uh-oh! Another disaster somewhere,* he thought.

As he relaxed back into his comfy armchair, the sirens got louder. Blue lights flashed, whizzing around the room. Suddenly, Blam! Blam! Blam! A flurry of car doors resonated through the house. He ran outside to see hordes of police swarming into his neighbours' house.

One officer approached Declan. 'Name, sir?'

'Declan Mitchell.'

'What are you doing here, sir?'

'Er ... I live here, at No. 9,' Declan said, pointing at his front door.

‘We received a call from a member of the public about a disturbance at your next-door neighbour’s—number 11. I’m sorry to have to inform you they have been . . . well, let’s say . . . they’re dead . . . murdered, most likely.’

‘My God! What! How? I didn’t hear a thing. I don’t know anything about it!’

‘Let’s finish this down at the station, sir. We need you to come with us.’

Without further enquiry, the officer marched a vehement, protesting Declan down the path to an awaiting police car, while a swarm of police officers cordoned off the entire street.

‘I know nothing about it, I tell you,’ he shouted. Declan’s protestations were ignored.

As they drove on, he fumbled in his pockets for his phone. No luck. All he could find was the doomed young girl’s necklace. *Oh my God,* he thought. *They’re going to blame me for the teenagers’ murders. So, the bastards will try to pin Shannon and Ronan’s murders on me, too!*

The police car sped on.

Back at No.11

'There's a dog hiding under here, Gov,' a cop called out. 'The little bugger's scared stiff and he don't look well. We'll need the dog handler.'

As if he wasn't traumatised enough, Spot found himself muzzled up and carted off to the kennels. After the police vet had calmed Spot down, they took samples from a single, red 4mm mark on his back.

It took only twenty-four hours for the results to come back, confirming that it was indeed the dead girls' blood. The same DNA fate met Declan concerning the victim's necklace that was found on him, linking him, one hundred per cent, to the crime scene.

Declan's next home would be at Her Majesty's pleasure. For Spot, it was the animal rescue centre. And yet, despite the horrors of the past, he sensed the promise of spring was in the air, giving the little Jack Russell renewed hope for a new, loving, ghost-free family ahead.

Chapter 6

Nosey Parker Meets Redneck

Residing at No. 7, next to Ronan, Shannon and Spot's old house, are the original, nosey neighbours.

From behind the curtains, they had watched the strange comings and goings of the last few weeks with mounting incredulity. They were aware the police had charged Declan with the murders of 'The Bodies in the Canal' and they found out from an acquaintance who worked at the nearby animal rescue centre that they had recently admitted Spot there.

They'd always had a soft 'spot' for that dog.

While taking a morning coffee break, ungluing themselves from the windows in search of the next bit of gossip, they decided to visit the rescue centre to enhance their sad existence with a dog of their own.

Spot was dozing in his new 'cell' when a kind assistant woke him gently.

'Here he is!' she said.

'Ooh, what a cutie! Isn't he, Dear?'

Mrs Parker's long-suffering, henpecked husband simply nodded in agreement, knowing that his answer was, as always, irrelevant.

Spot mused that he'd been called some things . . . but . . . a Cutie?

Mrs Nosey Parker came to a quick decision. 'We shall take him,' she announced. Spot felt a tad unsure about this unexpected, rapid development. All the shit he'd been through had instilled in him a healthy dose of scepticism but, hey ho. What the hell, bring it on!

Off they trundled in the grey, nondescript hatchback with She Who Must Be Obeyed barking out regular commands ranging from, 'Look out for that!' to 'You're going too fast!' Or, 'Get a move on, for God's sake!'

As their car pulled up outside No. 7, Spot felt mixed emotions. He'd experienced good and bad in this neck of the woods, but he decided he was fully prepared to give it another go. What choice did he have?

At first glance, Spot thought nothing in the neighbourhood had changed, but on closer observation, he noticed one difference to the otherwise familiar landscape. Backing onto the opposite side of the daisy-covered village green was a rickety fence marking the garden boundary of the big house. On the other side of the fence stood two antiquated-looking metal containers of considerable size, set off the ground a few feet. Spot absently dismissed this observation as his owners led him into his new home.

To be fair, 'er indoors and her chained-up guard dog of a husband were as good as gold to him. They gave him free rein to squeeze in and out of the dog-sized cat flap, he was more than well-fed, and his bed was warm and comfy. A world away from Sir and Lady Waster's hovel.

On one of his first solo walks, Spot found himself at the metal containers that he had noticed on his arrival. As he approached, a sizable rodent slithered out from underneath one of them and made for his rat hole yards away in the hedge. Spot thought his luck was in as he made chase. Scampering like mad, he got there . . . just as Ratty disappeared down his hole.

The next day, Mr Parker suggested to M'Lady his intention to take Spot out himself. 'Yes, well, don't lose him, for goodness' sake!' came the ungracious response. The suspicious-looking oil drums intrigued Parker.

'Yes, Dear,' was his outward, weary reply, while inside he was thinking of his only moments of satisfaction: taking the piss out of his wife when she had no idea he was doing so. He particularly loved his famous Thunderbirds one-liner, delivered with heavy sarcasm: 'Yes, M'Lady.'

Spot and Mr Parker arrived at the fence just as a 7.5-tonner was backing up the track leading to the gate in the rickety fence. The truck halted. A cheery chappy slid down from the cab and came across to them.

'Sorry if I startled you guys, but I just gotta drop off some stuff.'

He opened up the back, jumped in, got his pump truck and with the tail lift, proceeded to unload six rusty-looking 45-gallon drums, which he deposited next to the tanks.

Parker had to ask, 'Whatever is in those drums?'

The chatty driver immediately told him. 'Petrol—fuel for the boss man's pickup.'

With that, he climbed back into the driving seat and fired up the engine. Just as he reached the top of the track an American pickup truck turned in. Both drivers briefly wound down their windows and carried on. The butch-looking American truck, sporting a set of cattle horns on the front bumper, to emphasise the 'Good Old Boy' inclination of the obsessive owner, approached Parker and Spot.

The driver jumped down from the left-hand door, clanked it shut, and strolled up to them. 'And to what do I owe the pleasure?' he inquired.

Parker immediately fell on the defensive. 'Oh, we're just out for a walk. Love the vehicle,' he said.

This passive tack produced an immediate result. 'Well, y'all, both look after yourselves and have a good ol' day,' he drawled, in a heavy Texan accent, tipping his cowboy hat to them in the process.

'Full of shit, or what?' Parker muttered under his breath as the 'extravagance' guzzled back up the track. Parker could not wait to tell, 'er indoors.

As they retraced their steps home, he thought, *I should get Brownie points for this: who knows, I might even get a cup of tea!*

M'Lady was indeed impressed. A Jammy Dodger sat next to the steaming mug of tea on a decorative plate as they both surmised the cowboy's intentions.

Parker had it all worked out. 'That pickup uses copious amounts of petrol, so that first guy's going to keep bringing those drums from who-knows-where until our cowboy friend fills them all up.'

'Yes, but won't that present a fire risk?' M'Lady suggested. 'It's an accident waiting to happen, surely. It could go up like a World War Two bomb!'

'And then some,' Parker agreed.

Mrs Nosey Parker announced her intention to call the police first thing in the morning. *Fiddlesticks to, 'Have a Nice Day!'* she thought.

When she finally got through to the police, the responder churned out the familiar, patronising response,

'Sorry, Madam, we will get an officer to look into it, but it may take a little time.' Or, put another way, *get off the line and stop wasting our time.*

Mrs Parker sighed. 'Typical! Oh well, I tried.'

Chapter 7

Banged Up

Declan was in his new home: the cell he'd be sharing with three other inmates. It wasn't massive, but from what he'd gathered, it was a palace compared to other unfortunates' grim conditions. *Luck of the draw,* he guessed.

As time went on, he could see how prisoners could easily become institutionalised, not wanting to forgo this free-of-charge life.

He embraced life in the clink, joining the amateur boxing club—he'd always been handy with his fists—and the gym. As a result, his former roly-poly appearance became a thing of the past. If not yet sporting a six-pack, it was coming on.

One place he'd never set foot was a library, so when one of the screws suggested he visit the in-house facility, heavy scepticism loomed. Gingerly stepping through the door, he saw the librarian beavering away on her computer. He faked a cough. The librarian looked over her shoulder, stopped what she was doing and, with a sweet smile and easy charm, asked, 'How may I help you?'

Those cool grey-blue eyes captivated him, not sexually; he just felt a natural empathy could be on the cards. The Librarian's demeanour suggested she might agree.

Declan began to spend a good part of his days in the library. He discovered a love for reading, writing and other skills the librarian encouraged in him, including learning French. *Hmm* . . . he thought. Could come in handy on the beer run . . . if he ever got the chance to go on one again.

She smiled and said, 'Declan, you don't have to refer to me as Miss Librarian, you can call me Judy.'

'*D'accord*, Judy!' he countered, returning the smile. All this encouragement was doing wonders for his self-confidence.

Jacquie, the screw assigned to his cell, although physically attractive, spoke with a hard-as-nails South African accent. And when addressed, barked, 'Step out of line and you'll be dead meat.'

This no-nonsense approach, coupled with her I'll-give-you-a-chance-first attitude, bought her respect from most of the prisoners. She was affectionately known as Jack.

Declan, recognised by his altogether passive demeanour, occasionally enamoured his acquaintances. This masked the fact that, in reality, he was as hard as the displaced Afrikaner.

Over time, the predictable outcome unfolded: Declan and Jack met surreptitiously at first. Then, one day, finding themselves alone in the cell, they put their coffees down and gazed into each other's eyes. Hers, cold grey with lighter brown centres, reflecting a ruthless exterior, yet tempered by a compassionate interior. At once, they fell into each other's arms.

As they embraced, luxuriating in the *being so wrong but feeling so right* kind of way, Jack suddenly felt Declan physically changing, reducing in stature, right in front of her eyes. She backed off, just in time. Then, she too, like all the others before her, stood rooted to the spot, completely under the spell of Kayleigh, who stood in front of her now. There was no way Kayleigh would afford Declan any actual pleasure, especially of this sort. Kayleigh's initial visceral anger was immediately replaced with an insidious calmness as she excitedly anticipated the orgasmic climax to come. Caressing the hilt of her concealed weapon she raised her arm.

The cell door flew open, crashing against the wall. Jack seized the heaven-sent distraction and wrenching herself from her assailant, an impossible thought seared through her mind. She had believed him innocent, *was he a murderer after all?*

A screw stood in the doorway, panting, blood pouring from an ugly head wound. His eyes wild, he blurted out,

'Jack, the prisoners are rioting. They're threatening to burn the whole place down. Quick! Come on!'

Jack ran into the corridor with the other screw. She glanced back. Only Declan was standing there, the spell broken. Declan followed. Jack, feeling a compulsion to protect him.

Smoke billowed below the ceilings, the toxicity choking. The distant commotion rose to a crescendo as hordes of prisoners headed towards them, pushing fellow inmates out of the way and trampling others underfoot in their panic to get out.

Running down the corridor, Jack and Declan passed a rack of coats. Despite the bizarre incident in the cell, Jack trusted her instincts. Thinking ahead, she ripped one off its hook. She pulled Declan into an alcove. Breathing hard, pressed against each other, feeling each other's heartbeats, they waited to pick their moment to join the crazy exodus.

Now, at last, they were outside the building. The night sky glowed with roaring flames, all-consuming. Someone had opened the gates to prevent the situation from escalating.

'Take this coat, Declan! Go!' Jack yelled, tears welling up in her eyes.

He ran. He turned, 'I'll never forget you, Jack,' but she was gone, lost in the unfolding chaotic scenes.

Declan had to get a grip. He had to focus. Or all that would have been for nothing. He needed transport.

Luckily, he knew the area like the back of his hand. Sloughing off his prison garb, he put on the coat Jack had thrust into his arms. Fighting the temptation to run, he settled into a fast walk, heading off towards a built-up area. Passing a bin, he dumped his prison clothes. Arriving at a set of traffic lights, his hastily devised plan was to wait until a dodgy-looking character pulled up at the lights.

In due course, a promising candidate screeched to a halt, the loud music boom-booming. A hoody sat behind the wheel, smoking what looked like a joint. He was looking around, left and right, in a guilty-as-hell manner.

Banging on the driver's door, 'Get out! NOW!' Declan screamed, wrenching it open.

He grabbed the hoody, yanked him out and pulled him to the ground. As the stunned driver got up he whipped out a four-inch blade and pointed it at Declan, a smug smile now crossing his face. In a split second, Declan clattered the knife to the road. If the first solid body blow to the sternum took that smile away, the following vicious uppercut to the chin almost took his head off. The hoody crashed to the ground, out for the count.

Leaving him in a heap in the middle of the road, Declan jumped into the driver's seat just as the lights were changing. *Should've used that blasted knife,* he thought. Flooring the accelerator, the car flew forward, tyres screeching. He mentally calculated an ETA of about twenty minutes to his former house.

Chapter 8

Free at Last

Racing along—this hatch was hot! Declan's dry throat cried out for a drink. Looking across to the passenger seat, he spotted an open multipack of Red Bull nestling in the footwell. *Yeah, result!* With a considerable bit of manipulation, the first was downed in one, the second only marginally slower. By the time he'd finished the fourth, the effects of the quick-acting energy drinks kicked in.

'How the hell do I switch that damned racket off?' He jabbed a finger at the radio while trying to keep the car in a straight line with the other hand. Instantly, the boom-boom was replaced by a more melodic, 'Alright, baby now. It's alright ...' He knew this song—one of his favourite bands—Free. The irony was not lost on him. He sang along, knowing the lyrics by heart.

Ten minutes to go.

He drove faster, taking the racing line around the corners, discovering driving skills he didn't know he had. He was Max Verstaffen, heading for the chequered flag.

Five minutes to go.

The dreaded voice in his head spoke to him again. Kayleigh. 'It's no good, Declan, it's not Alright Now. I've told you before, you will never be free.'

The song on the still-blaring radio changed. This time, 'In Too Deep,' Belinda Carlisle. Declan was losing it. It seemed the Kayleigh Being had won. Inextricably, he was doomed to a living hell.

He knew now he couldn't go on like this.

Two minutes to go.

He gulped down another Red Bull in desperation: the balance of his mind buckled beyond repair.

'Faster!' ordered Max V.

'Slower!' countered Kayleigh.

Declan, all-consumed by the Being, shrieked with a voice he did not recognise,

'Shut up! Shut the fuck up!'

The car screeched around the last bend.

Spot was out by the petrol drums again, hunting in vain for Ratty, when he heard the roar of a fast-approaching car, its dazzling beams momentarily freezing him like a rabbit in the headlights. Coming to his senses, Spot knew he had to get the hell out of there. He shot across the road, forcing Declan to take evasive action. As the car swerved past, narrowly missing him, Spot caught a glimpse of the driver. Declan panicked. He hit the brakes. Big mistake—it was the accelerator. The car lurched forward, striking the kerb. And as he flew up into the air, heading straight for those accident-waiting-to-happen petrol tanks, Declan's life flashed before him as a shimmering grey ether drifted into the sky. The vehicle and its contents vaporised instantly. The tremendous flash flicked night to day.

Spot was reaching the back garden of a random house when flying red-hot shrapnel and all manner of debris shot past him, hitting the wooden fence, and catching it alight.

He ran for cover, putting a safe distance between him and the conflagration. He waited. He didn't know for how long.

When he thought it was safe, still trembling with shock, he dared to peek out from his hiding place. All that remained of the vehicle and its contents were pieces of twisted metal and a pile of white, smouldering ash. Thick acrid smoke filled the air—devastation all around.

Spot wondered who could have survived that.

Obviously not Declan, but ...?

Suddenly, Spot felt that familiar chill. He knew what was coming. Holding his nerve, thinking only positive thoughts, he resolved that this time it would be different. He understood the principle that fear is the key, so he vowed not to show an iota. He owed this much to Declan. The chill lingered.

Come on, Spot, resist! he repeated to himself.

The chill finally relented. Spot knew he'd won.

The area soon filled up with shocked residents. The emergency services swung into action, blue lights flashing and sirens whining, their vehicles disgorging troops of service personnel, dashing about, attempting to make some sense out of it all. For Spot, it was time to pick his way around the smouldering debris and make his way home.

Back on his comfy bed, he took stock of what had happened. He had inadvertently liberated Declan. And stood up to the Being. After all the tension, he felt a state of mind previously unknown—a rare feeling of euphoria. *So that's what cloud nine feels like,* he thought.

Kayleigh was livid. The incident had exposed her powers as something less than all-encompassing. The prison cell debacle was a massive disappointment, and then *that dog* unexpectedly fought back!

In the future, when identifying her next victim, she would have to select an easier target. She already knew the likely attributes the chosen new Being should possess. Vanity, cockiness, arrogance and insecurity. And bigoted, for good measure. Perfect.

She acknowledged, however, that the chances of this happening overnight were slim. But then, she was not in a rush. She had all the time in the world.

And her patience . . . infinite.

Part Two

Chapter 9

Everyone Loves a Pretty Girl

Beep—beep—beep. The incessant sound occupied a remote segment of his inner mind. His eyelids fluttered fitfully, and as his brain attempted to re-engage, an overwhelming, uninvited fear invaded every atom of his awakening being. That was enough for now.

As he began to drift, he thought he saw the image of a dog. And then, he felt himself being swept along, only to be brutally dumped and left to his fate. He felt his muscles twitch, and on the verge of losing control, he sunk back into welcome unconsciousness.

Nurse Catherine, or Cat as everyone knew her, loved her job despite the long hours and nonstop schedule. All the clichés about job satisfaction and wanting to make a difference were, in Cat's case, true. She stood by the side of the hospital bed for a few minutes to make sure her bandaged, unidentifiable, totally messed up patient was stable. *What would his chances be?* As her eyes darted back and forth between the indifferent beeping machines and the patient, she had a strange feeling that she knew him.

His records were surprisingly brief, simply stating that the emergency services attended an RTA involving a vehicle colliding at high speed with a fuel store. The explosion destroyed the car. An unexplained 50 metres from the scene, the police found one unconscious body, suffering extensive injuries but still clinging to life. There was no ID, and his face was burned beyond recognition.

Cat replaced the notes, privately speculating, *what the hell had gone on here and why was the victim so far away from the crash scene?* Something just didn't feel right. She returned to check the monitors, knowing that when she left, the array of warning lights and buzzers would alert someone, just in case of any unexpected deviations from the established parameters. As far as the saintly Catherine was concerned, whatever lay in wait for this guy in the future, he would receive the best professional treatment to aid his recovery. For some reason, she felt an obligation to help him.

With these perplexing thoughts in her mind, she headed off to check on the next patient, and the one after that. The ICU was always busy.

Cat looked at her watch. Time for her break. But on her way to that well-deserved cuppa, she hesitated—deciding to look in on her new patient.

Satisfied that he appeared stable, she left, thinking, *I ought to give him a name, or an initial, at least. Err ... I think I'll call him Liam. It means strong-willed warrior. That'll suit him fine.*

That cuppa beckoned. But just as Cat was about to push open the door to thirty minutes of freedom, all hell broke loose. Warning buzzers pierced the air. She turned her head. It was the ICU! Hurrying back, Cat could see Liam was struggling to breathe. She hardly needed to check on his oxygen saturation level, it was dropping fast.

Below 80% would mean big trouble. Acting swiftly, yet remaining calm, Cat attached the ventilator breathing tube. Holding her breath, she watched the readings as Liam's oxygen level crept up steadily.

Whew! That was a close call.

She hardly noticed the ICU consultant. 'Everything under control here? Hmm ... good ... looks like it,' Naresh said. Cat explained what had just occurred, suspecting that

'Great! Everything's looking good,' she said with a relieved sigh. Moving in close and looking intently into Liam's bandaged face, she whispered, 'You're an enigma, for sure, sweetheart. Who are you, for goodness' sake? And how on earth did you get into this mess?'

And with that, she handed over to the on-duty nurses and made her way home.

Cat had moved into her park-side flat only a few months earlier. At the start, she enjoyed the challenge of putting her imaginative interior design skills to the test. But that was done. And it was at this moment, pretty much every day, that she experienced an unwelcome surge of apprehension at the prospect of going back home. A home devoid of any significant other. As she pushed the key into the keyhole, turning it slowly, listening for the metallic clicks, her irrational nervousness returned.

Despite the inevitable end-of-shift exhaustion, Cat rued what might follow. Sometimes she'd be unsettled for nights on end, sometimes not. Tonight, Cat decided it would be a good night. She was determined about that.

'Sod it!' she announced, grabbing her coat. 'I'm going out to Abduls. I need a bottle of Chardonnay and fresh, crusty bread. Yes! The cheese and those cherry tomatoes have been in the fridge for a couple of days, at least. They definitely need finishing off! And maybe a Turkish Delight after that. To hell with those carbs!'

Cat felt life owed her this moment of self-indulgence. *So why not?*

As she crossed the park on the way to Abdul's Emporium, an observing Being breathed, 'Why not indeed.'

Returning home, she turned the key quickly, stepped back in, dumped her coat on the floor and headed for the kitchen. Slap-up meal ready, she snuggled back onto her cosy settee, tray on lap, wine at hand.

'Right!' she announced. 'Now for the re-run of Heart-beat. My favourite.' She sipped her wine as the incidental music transported her back to the Sixties, the fictional series set in the North Yorkshire Moors—a local police officer, his GP wife and their adventures.

Cat soaked up the scenery, the down-to-earth characters and the return to a bygone age where politics, as yet, had not taken over every aspect of life.

Cat's cousin lived near Gromont; a village frequently featured in the classic series. He hadn't seen her since he'd moved up there. Over the phone and by email, he had implored her to come up and stay at any time; and for as long as she liked. And Cat knew these weren't merely hollow words—he meant it. She bit into her crusty bread, not caring that the settee looked as if it had suddenly developed dandruff.

Cat suddenly had a premonition, of sorts. The vision of a crumbly stone house by the side of a babbling brook came into her head and then faded. *Might she be taking up his offer in the not-too-distant future?* The enticing prospect intrigued Cat. And anyway, who wouldn't want to move from the grime of the city to that idyllic bolt-hole? Suddenly, Belinda Carlyle's, 'Heaven is a Place on Earth' popped into her mind. And then, mid-munch, she thought of Liam. Somehow, having survived his brush with death so far, this song, although not of a *Heartbeat* ilk, seemed appropriate.

Cat reflected on her day as she tidied up and got ready for bed. She promised herself only optimism from now on. So, with all negative feelings banished for a change, and only pleasant thoughts in her head, she instantly fell into a contented slumber.

And yet, an otherworldly Being looked down at her, *So you're the Miss Goodie-Goodie Two Shoes, looking after my shrivelled-up, former host. Why don't you let him die? I'll have to keep an eye on you, girly.*

In the morning, the soft-toned alarm eased Cat awake. *God! What's the time?* She reached for her phone.

'Oh, it's only 6 o'clock.' And as she came to her senses, Cat realised what a wonderful sleep she'd had. *That's the best I've had since I moved in. I reckon it's going to be a good day. Time to get moving.*

She showered, dressed, brushed her luxurious shock of red hair and applied a minimal amount of makeup. The hospital and another day with her rapidly developing obsession—her new patient—awaited. She was out of the house like a whirlwind, banging the door behind her while thanking her lucky stars she had the job of her dreams.

The Being noted the young woman's understated beauty and extreme positivity. Then, it felt a mix of emotions: excitement and trepidation in roughly equal measures. *Everyone loves a pretty girl,* it thought.

And was Cat pretty—not perhaps in a purely conventional way—it was just that anyone who met her felt a natural attraction. They wanted to be with her. This, Cat discovered years ago, afforded her the deliciously effortless ability to get her own way. Naturally, it often infuriated those inadequate in the department. They were simply and often insanely envious.

Cat's singular talent resonated with the Being. I wonder if she could be useful in the future; it conjectured. And yet, there was the outside possibility that this potential, wily adversary might not be the pushover that the Being preferred.

No matter. A plan would be required for this eventuality. In the meantime, the Being would continue to bide its time—as always.

Chapter 10

I Don't Believe This

Cat glanced up at a darkening sky, wondering if she would make the five-minute walk to the hospital before the heavens opened. In her haste, she'd forgotten her umbrella, and there was no time to go back and get it. As her workplace came into view, the first ominous drops fell; the wind markedly picked up.

'Oh dear!' she muttered. Within seconds, Cat was drenched.

As she crossed the car park, she noticed more blue flashing lights than usual. And it seemed a few were marked police cars. *What's going on?*

She crashed through the entrance door of the hospital atrium, glad to be out of the unexpected monsoon. *Why were there no patients milling around?*

A uniformed police officer appeared out of nowhere. 'Can I see your ID, madam?' was his swift enquiry, standing right in front of her in an intimidating manner.

'Why, yes, of course!'

Cat fumbled to undo her sopping-wet coat, finally revealing her tag to the persistent, suspicious copper towering over her.

He scrutinised the information and immediately backed off from a relieved Cat.

'That's fine, madam,' he said, his tone softening. 'Off you go to carry on your important work. Thanks for your cooperation.'

Thanks for that! she thought.

More than intrigued, Cat dumped her dripping coat, tidied herself up in the washroom, and made her way to the ICU. As she arrived at the door, another officer jumped up from his seat to challenge her. *Jeepers, whatever is happening?* she thought. Again, meticulously examining her tag, the officer decided she was the genuine article. He opened the door to let her in, immediately shutting it behind her.

Cat approached Liam's bed, passing Naresh, the consultant who was deep in conversation with two high-ranking police officers, and two other anxious-looking individuals—a man exploiting a no-nonsense demeanour and an equally don't-mess-with-me woman, all conducting themselves in a carefully rehearsed professional manner. Cat checked Liam and his monitors; all seemed fine. At that moment, Naresh appeared at her side. The heavies had departed the room. He looked into her eyes with not a little concern.

Naresh took a deep breath and with a swift recce of the room, whispered, 'Come on, nurse! We'd better continue this in the privacy of my office.'

Cat followed dutifully, feeling wary and apprehensive of what Naresh might reveal. He clicked the office door shut, having instructed the guarding officer outside the ICU ward to forbid any unnecessary interruptions. Sitting down, he gathered his thoughts while Cat seated herself to face him. She could hardly wait—the tension was palpable.

'Nurse!' Mr Hussain said at last, 'Those people who I was talking to just now are from the police and the prison service. They have produced DNA results confirming our patient's identity. It seems he was the inmate who escaped from that dreadful fire at the prison a few days ago. Do you remember? It's been all over the media.'

'Yes, yes, Mr Hussain, of course,' spluttered Cat.

'Well,' continued Naresh, 'our patient is that very person. His name is Declan Mitchell.'

'Goodness!' Cat breathed. 'And what was his crime?'

Naresh had to tell her what he knew she wouldn't want to hear. He paused …'double murder …of two teenage girls.

an infection was the cause. Naresh checked the readings. 'Good, well done, nurse! Keep up the good work.'

'Thank you, Mr Hussain,' Cat replied, allowing herself a satisfied smile. It was gratifying to be valued.

Consultant Naresh undeniably held Cat in the highest regard. Returning her smile, he privately acknowledged his and the facility's good fortune in having such a reliable, efficient member of staff. He was also relieved personnel of her calibre took the pressure off him. Naresh Hussein was an unsung hero of this department. He never unduly criticised his staff, confident in delegating responsibility to those he trusted to be allowed to get on with their job. Cross him, and that was a different matter. If you can't deliver, you're out!

The medics put Liam on a two-week course of antibiotics, hoping that this would clear the infection. By that time, if no other major problem reared its head, they would take him out of the ICU and transfer him to a general ward. Of course, there was the ongoing matter of his not-inconsiderable injuries and burns to his face, but that was under control.

For the rest of her shift, Cat made sure to keep an eye on her new, unidentified patient, Liam.

It was way past Cat's clocking-off time, as usual. She took one last look at Liam's monitors.

And they suspect he did his neighbours in, as well. Although the police have found no evidence, yet.'

Cat sat for a while, digesting this unbelievable news. Despite having come into contact with her new patient only recently, her instincts told her this couldn't be true. And Cat trusted her instincts. More than ever now, Liam, aka Declan, needed her help. She vowed to continue to provide it, no matter what, no question at all. Mr Hussain's visitors had certainly raised eyebrows and whisperings among the staff. But having been warned by the management team not to breathe a word about their convict patient, the hospital quickly reverted to its usual functioning. Considering Declan's condition, he could hardly abscond. However, the serious nature of the convicted murderer's crime required a police guard outside the ICU, 24/7.

Declan raised his heavy eyelids slowly. He forced himself to concentrate. 'Oh my God, where am I? How did I get here? Who the hell am I?'

Cat's calm face appeared in front of him. Instantly, his extreme apprehension and utter panic subsided.

'Hello, there! I'm Nurse Catherine, and your name is Declan. You've been involved in an accident, but we, at this wonderful hospital, are going to make you better.' Declan seemed to take this in, gradually closing his eyes to rest again after this exhausting first step back to the land of the living.

Cat felt a rush of optimism. 'Looks like he's on the road to recovery, thanks to you.' Naresh said, arriving at her side.

'Well, the entire team has excelled. And yes, I believe he is,' agreed Cat.

Cat was passing the ICU nursing station when the receptionist called her over. 'Nurse Catherine! Mr Hussain would like to see you in his office as soon as you are free.'

'Okay, I can go now. Could you phone to say I am on my way, please?'

Cat stepped up to the consultant's door and knocked gently.

'Come!' ordered Naresh.

Cat sidled in, pinning the wayward strands of her red hair into submission.

'Ah, nurse! Thank you for taking the time. Take a seat; now then ... just a second,' he said, accessing his computer.

'Ah, yes, here it is.' He looked up at her. 'The prison service has sent some vital information through regarding Declan. Fortunately, the information they have supplied appears more thorough than can sometimes be the case in these situations.' Cat nodded.

Naresh adjusted the screen to allow both of them to see the text. He read it out.

On admission, Liam underwent a psychological assessment. From the outset, he protested his innocence at the charges levelled against him, making it abundantly clear he considered himself a victim of circumstance. When invited to provide his view of the events leading up to the murder of the two girls, he could not answer, citing loss of memory. However, although there was no other evidence, the DNA results placed him definitively at the scene of the crime.

'No other evidence? That sounds a bit tenuous, don't you think?' Cat offered.

'Yes, it does. I agree. There's more ...'

'Rather than remaining resentful toward his captors, Liam positively embraced prison life, joining several activities, including the gym, the amateur boxing club and the library. No misdemeanours were recorded and when questioned, all members of staff reported he presented as the unusual example they all yearned for—pleasant and courteous—a model prisoner.'

Silence!

Naresh looked over at Cat with a raised eyebrow. 'Nurse?'

'Well, not that I have much experience with these things, but his demeanour doesn't appear to be that of a cold-blooded killer of two young girls. At least, not to me,' Cat ventured.

'My thoughts entirely. And although we have to take their assessment into account, above everything else the Hippocratic Oath dictates it is our job to rehabilitate our patients. So that is what we will continue to do. Agreed, Nurse Catherine?'

'Agreed.'

'Okay, nurse, carry on!'

As Cat opened the door, she turned. 'Thank you, Mr Hussain.'

He smiled his reply.

Feeling elated, Cat made tracks for the canteen. Over a coffee, she reflected on the revelation she had shared with Naresh. Her unequivocal trust in Declan might possibly be vindicated. Someone had set this guy up for something he probably hadn't done. That was pretty damned obvious. But how could this apparent miscarriage of justice be rectified? Cat had no idea. But whatever transpired in the future, she would continue to do her utmost to fix him, regardless. What else could she do?

The Being was troubled. *Declan must remain guilty. I have to stop Miss Goodie-Goodie Two Shoes.*

Chapter 11

Canine Possibilities

Declan's steady progress surprised everyone. Naresh and his team transferred him into a private room adjoining the general ward, where he could continue his recovery. The logistics complete, Cat realised she would not be seeing so much of her treasured patient from now on. She would, of course, pop in regularly. Instead, the attractive young nurse standing in front of her would assume responsibility for looking after Cat's prodigy.

The bubbly nurse announced, 'Hi Cat, I've heard a lot about you!'

'Not all bad, I hope!'

They laughed, instantly breaking the ice. Cat glanced at this effervescent new colleague's tag.

‘And you are Roxette! That sounds like a fun-loving name.’

‘You bet!’ came the confident reply.

Cat just knew they would get on like the proverbial house on fire.

As Cat left, glancing back at the still unconscious Declan, she said, ‘Hey, Roxette! I’ll see you on our break if you like, and we can discuss Declan in more detail. I’ve got to get back to the ICU now before they miss me.’

‘Great, Cat! I’ll see you later.’

And Cat was gone, passing the bored-as-hell, dozy police officer, ostensibly guarding the absconded killer.

Distractedly picking up her tray of light refreshments, Cat scanned the canteen for her new pal. Got her in a flash! As she made her way across to the table, Cat took in Roxette’s dark wavy hair, easy constant smile and modestly proportioned figure. Cat liked what she saw. As she sat down, the same thoughts went through Roxette’s mind.

They were enjoying their snack when the Declan conundrum came up. Cat updated his new curator with the technical stuff, which she immediately took on board. ‘The rumour mill has gone into overdrive in this hospital,’ Roxette said, hazel eyes sparkling. ‘Your hero status reputation, before all this kicked off, has now risen to the Patron Saint of Lost Causes!' All they could do was giggle.

'I've got a tough act to follow!' Roxette said, catching her breath.

'You'll be fine. Wow! Look at the time! Hey, we've got to get a wiggle on!' Cat pushed her chair back, but as she got up, she hesitated. 'Roxette, how do you fancy coming round to my place one night to help me demolish a bottle of Chardonnay or two?'

'You're on!'

After yet another exhausting day, Cat slumped down onto her settee, thinking she needed company in her life— maybe of the canine variety. Her landlord was a great guy who was unlikely to object, so long as the place didn't get wrecked. And she would walk the dog, morning and night, on the canal just around the corner from her flat.

She got up, poured herself a modest glass of wine and set up her computer to search for her likely companion online. 'Pets to Love'. Hmm ... sounds interesting. She clicked on it. A sizable list of pooches appeared, from Chihuahuas to Great Danes.

I need to narrow this down. 'Let's try ... Jack Russell.' Result! One advert took her eye.

‘Free to a good home. Was a cutie; now in need of a little TLC?’

And there was a picture of him, all snowy white with a big black spot in the middle of his back. Cat was smitten. *I’ll ring the number now,* she said to herself, positivity to the fore, as always.

A female voice answered almost immediately. ‘Hello, can I help you?’

Cat asked the usual stuff—Did he have any ailments? How old was he? And so on. She didn’t want a puppy that might destroy her flat on day one.

‘Oh, not at all, dear, he’s a mature little fellow!’ the voice on the other end said. ‘Come over and see him. I’m sure you’ll love him.’

Cat agreed, and they settled on the following Saturday: Cat’s day off.

‘Okay, see you then, dear.’

Cat wasn’t sure about the moniker, ‘dear’, though.

The next day, in a quieter moment, Cat stole away to check on Declan. As she opened the door to the private room, the police guard staggered to his feet, papers flying everywhere, obviously rudely awoken. Cat showed him her ID. Satisfied, he sat down to return to his bored slumber.

Declan was finally conscious. Cat looked into his blue eyes. He tried to smile, but it didn't really work. Cat thought he looked more like a human being now rather than an Egyptian mummy. It was a good sign. He tried again. This time, his smile did just about work.

The door opened, and in rocked Roxette, still smiling that infectious smile. The two nurses discussed the patient and his continuing good progress.

'Roxette, I have to go back to ICU but ...'

'Yep?'

'What are you doing Friday night—how do you fancy coming round to my place for that drink?'

'Yeah, love to. Text me the address. Eight o'clock?'

'Done!'

It was 20.01 when Cat heard the tap-a-tap of her door knocker. She opened the door to see Roxette underneath a dripping umbrella but still managing to look fabulous.

'Hey, Roxette! Come on in out of that horrible rain.'

Roxette slowly took off her coat to reveal a quite plain but oh-so-well-fitting red and white dogtooth shift dress that showed off her modest curves to perfection.

'Wow! You look fab,' observed a stunned Cat, not sure if she was ready to be *innamorato,* just yet.

'You too,' Roxette complimented, admiring her beautiful icon, adorned in a white faux leather skirt and loosely fitting, black silk top.

Coming to her senses, Cat ushered her new friend onto the expansive settee. 'Now, let's get serious: red or white?'

Roxette laughed, 'White, please!'

Cat placed the two glasses on the very occasional table where they were easily at hand. They chatted as though they had known each other for years.

'Mm, this wine is fab,' Roxette pronounced. It was time for another bottle.

Cat decided to tell Roxette about her plan to get a dog. Excitedly, she fired up the laptop to reveal the details of her proposed furry flatmate.

'Look here, Roxette! It says, *Was a cutie, now in need of some TLC.* What d'you think?'

'Sounds ominous, Cat? God! It might turn out to be a wild, rabid monster!' They fell about giggling; the alcohol having the usual effect.

'I'm going to check him out tomorrow, Roxy. You don't mind me calling you Roxy, do you?'

'Not at all. My friends call me that. Do you want me to come with you? It's my day off tomorrow as well, and we can't afford to lose the Patron Saint of Lost Causes to a canine catastrophe!'

Wow! This chick is switched on! Cat silently acknowledged. More giggling. More wine. It was getting late. Cat coughed, feeling a sudden frog in her throat.

'Are you okay?' Roxy asked.

'I've always had a small chest problem.'

'Looks alright to me.' The hopeless giggles began again, the drink now easing what few inhibitions they may have harboured.

Recovering themselves, they shuffled closer together on the settee. As much as Roxy appreciated Catherine's ever-present enthusiasm, her own philosophy was equally optimistic: believing everything works out fine. It was certainly looking that way!

They were up close now, staring into each other's eyes. Roxy's hazel and playful, Cat's dark, bottomless pools.

Cat thought, Heaven really is a Place on Earth, as they spontaneously fell into each other's arms. Instinctively, Cat whispered, 'Time for bed?'

A breathless Roxy agreed, 'Oh! I think so.'

Cat flicked the lock on the front door as they made their way upstairs, Roxy tripping up the top step, Cat crashing into her, the uncontrollable giggles starting again.

'First on the left!'

They fell through the bedroom doorway, where the king-sized bed, with the duvet folded back, beckoned. The would-be lovers rapidly dropped their clothes to the floor as they jumped in, pulling the duvet up to their chins. Turning to face one another, they gently embraced, drowning in the eroticism of this delicious and unusual scenario. These were precious moments to savour. And who knows? This chance might not come around again.

Finally, they fell back onto the downy pillows, their bodies floating in an ethereal place before falling into satisfied slumber.

The Being observed the scene, achingly seething, insanely jealous but powerless to disturb the intense magnetism of the two lovers. There would be trouble, it promised, be it sooner or later, but always at a time of its own desire and choosing.

Cat opened her eyes. Someone was breathing next to her. She felt a jolt of panic, but it was okay, of course. It all came back to her. Even allowing for the quantity of wine consumed, the events of last night were crystal clear in her mind. And she loved it. Cat got out of bed quietly, without disturbing the sleeping angel, Roxette. Pulling on her dressing gown, she made her way downstairs to put the coffee machine on.

'Crikey,' muttered the mistress of understatement as she surveyed the wreckage of the night before. She started tidying up while she waited for the saviour to produce the antidote.

Cat unearthed a small tray and carefully headed back to the scene of the 'crime'. Roxy was sitting up, looking bedraggled and not a little confused, breathing, 'Did that really happen, or did we just have far too much wine?'

'Both,' confirmed Cat, as they once again fell into agreeable laughter. Sipping their hot drinks, rather than suffering from guilt and embarrassment, they merely felt a natural empathy, not really wanting it to end—and why should it? As they finished their coffee, Cat reminded Roxy of their appointment with the Dangerous Dog that morning. 'Can't wait, Cat. After we've showered, can we stop off at my house so I can change into something more suitable for taming a potential wolf?'

'Ha-ha! Of course.'

Chapter 12

The Jack Russell

Cat backed her electric Zoe out of the garage at the back of the flats, noting the battery-level light displayed fully charged, which would easily take them there and back.

Roxy had walked the short distance to her flat. Cat pulled up outside. As she waited for Roxy, she pulled up the destination details on her phone. It was a Mr and Mrs Parker. She punched the rest of the information into the satnav on the car—it was easier and safer than fiddling with the phone. Twenty-nine minutes was the ETA.

Roxy slid into the passenger seat, placing her phone on the dash, and they were off. After all the rain of recent days, today the sun took control. As the electric car silently drove on, they both slipped into their new, also silent, comfort zone, privately rerunning the previous night's momentous events through their heads. Cat put her hand on Roxy's knee, squeezing it gently. Roxy reciprocated. They exchanged peaceful, knowing smiles.

Cat rang the doorbell, at the precise time agreed with Mrs Parker. 'Ooh! Thank you for being so prompt,' the otherwise bored wife said, opening the door. 'It's Cat, isn't it? Come on in!' She didn't admit she'd been waiting behind the curtains for twenty minutes in anticipation of actually seeing somebody new! 'Yes, and this is my friend Roxy,' replied Cat as their host led them in.

'Now, dear, I have to be honest,' Mrs Parker began.

Uh-oh! Roxy thought.

The lady noticed this slight negativity, but continued, 'Before I show you into the kitchen to meet Spot, I have to warn you he hasn't been himself for quite some time now and he can occasionally become a little bit, err . . . agitated.'

Roxy's face was a picture. *Are we on a wild goose chase here?* she wondered. Cat remained composed.

'Ready?' asked Mrs Parker. She opened the kitchen door to reveal the wild rabid monster that was Spot, sitting on his comfy bed with a squeaky toy next to him. Roxy looked at Cat. Cat looked at Mrs Parker. Mrs Parker said nothing.

A man entered the room. 'Hello! You must be Cat. You've met Spot, then.'

Mrs Parker pointed out to her husband that she'd warned the girls to be careful. Spot was already on the alert. He had pricked up his ears at the loud voices in the next room, and true enough, as soon as all these humans approached his territorial dog basket, he dropped his jaw and let out a low, guttural growl.

'I'll get him some biscuits to see if that will placate him.' Mr Parker suggested. He fished in a draw, pulled out some treats and held them out to Spot. There was a rack of precariously balanced saucepans behind him. Spot, anticipating trouble, snarled and pointedly placed a paw on the edge of the basket as a warning to deter this first potential adversary.

Mr Parker panicked, immediately falling backwards, crashing into the saucepans and scattering them across the ceramic floor tiles like ten-pin bowling pins.

Roxy had also taken two steps back. Cat waited for a few moments before taking slow steps closer to the rabid monster. The Parkers and Roxy watched in disbelief as Cat lent down to the dog, holding her hand out so he could sniff it. Spot's ears went down, and his eyes took on a sorrowful look as if to say, *I'm sorry about that, you know what it's like.*

Cat looked directly into Spot's eyes and silently replied, 'I know.' With that, she stroked his head, whereupon he looked back at her as if to say, *Thank you.*

There was an immediate connection between them, and yet Spot's nose detected an unexpected scent on her. A medicinal smell, yes, but also the scent of a man. A man from the past.

'It's a miracle,' declared Mrs Parker.

'Cat does miracles,' Roxy interjected.

'Obviously! Gosh!' Mrs Parker said. 'Let's leave him in peace for a bit. I'll put the kettle on and tell you a bit more about him. I'm assuming you want him after that performance?'

'Yes,' was Cat's simple answer.

Back in the lounge, Mrs Parker explained the reasons behind Spot's changed character. 'There was a horrific car crash which caused a massive amount of damage and destruction to the area. Spot must have been in the vicinity, because in the aftermath, when he bolted through his dog flap, he settled onto his bed looking . . . somehow different. Afterwards, he seemed fine for a while, venturing out, as he'd previously done, to hunt for Ratty and to attend to other dog-related matters. But over time, he went out less frequently, until it got to the point where he refused to shift from his bed at all, apart from the odd toilet visit.'

'And you think it was the shock of the crash that spooked him?' Roxy ventured.

'Oh, absolutely. I contacted the vet. He said it was probably—oh, that phrase I always forget—Pet Dramatic Dog Disorder or something like that.'

Sniggers stifled; Mr Parker marvelled at his wife's unfailing knack of showing herself up at every available opportunity.

'Well, dear, are you sure you still want him— seriously?' asked Mrs Parker. 'He may become a problem for you.'

Cat assured her she could handle him but offered to keep in touch to advise on progress. Mr Parker, on the other hand, found it hard to disguise a more cynical expression. But then, he would, wouldn't he? Roxy, noticing this giveaway, felt essentially non-committed but would naturally stand by her friend's judgement.

'Can I leave it to you to get him into the pet carrier?' Mrs Parker pleaded to the prospective new owner.

Cat replied, 'I'll try to put him directly on the back seat of the car, but I would be grateful for the carrier if you don't want it.'

Cat approached the dog basket, the audience holding its collective breath, as Cat knelt down in front of Spot. Speaking gently, she said, 'Spot, I'm going to take you away to come and live with me now.'

She waited for a response. The dog repeated that sad look that seemed to say, *Okay*.

'I'm going to lift you up and take you to my car. Are you okay with that?'

Spot's ears went down in submission. Cat slowly lifted him out of the basket and settled him into her arms. They all went out of the house.

'Can you open the back door to the car, Roxy?'

Cat deposited the little Jack Russell carefully onto the already prepared blanket on the back seat. Spot curled up immediately, his little face wearing a canine look of relief. Mr Parker was entranced, simply mouthing, job done!

They exchanged goodbyes with the Parkers. Mrs Parker called out after them, 'Good luck!'

And then they were gone.

Roxy was incredulous, but couldn't hold back from stating the obvious. 'Well, Cat, your legendary status as the Patron Saint of Lost Causes is still very much intact.'

'Love you, Babe!'

Roxy turned to check on the rabid monster. He had fallen asleep—a contented aura about him.

'Maybe it will be alright in the end,' the optimist ventured.

Chapter 13

The Shop

They turned into the street before their block of flats, Cat pulling up outside an old-fashioned corner shop.

'I've never been in here before,' she pointed out to Roxy. 'Although someone told me a new owner had recently taken the business over.'

'God, I hope it's run better now than it used to be,' Roxy hissed. 'They were a miserable husband and wife team regularly throwing the goods across the counter at you, then demanding payment with menaces!'

'I'd heard that, too!' Cat chuckled. 'Somebody told me the strange daughter might take it over because her parents were both retiring. God knows.'

'Nobody went there in the end,' Roxy continued, 'so it came as no surprise the business went under—if that's what's happened.'

'Oh well, all I need is some food for Spot. Wish me luck! Are you going to be okay with the wild rabid monster lurking in the back?'

Roxy glanced over her shoulder at the still-slumbering dog. 'Yeah, yeah,' Roxy replied, frowning a strained smile at Cat while secretly trying to convince herself.

Spot flinched as Cat closed the car door. He peered out of the back window and watched his new carer go into the shop. Pinning back his ears, he let out a guttural growl.

Cat walked through the narrow front entrance, expecting a pokey establishment, but she was amazed to discover that the shop opened up like the fictional TARDIS. It seemed anything was available here: from pear cider to Chardonnay wine. Nail files to kitchen knives.

'Can I help you?' a charming voice asked.

Taken aback by this instant attention, Cat spluttered, 'O-oh yes, please. I've just collected my very first pet dog. He'll need a bowl and some food. I must admit to feeling a bit out of my depth in this new role of pet parent.'

The shopkeeper recognised the stunning young woman as soon as she entered the shop. A degree of manipulation was now called for. Realising the engaging novice needed some help and sensing an opportunity, the shopkeeper smiled.

'Wait here ... '

'Oh, I'm Cat.'

'Nice to meet you, Cat. Just wait here a moment and I'll see what I can find.' She returned in no time, armed with a basic selection of dog food, biscuits and other pet-related paraphernalia.

Scanning the inventory, an amazed Cat gushed her thanks. 'Wow! That is so kind and helpful!'

While she waited for the card machine to process the payment, Cat looked across at the presumed new owner, dressed in an in-your-face black-and-white combination. Not yet appreciating this hint of her personality, Cat merely noted the name on her professional tag.

'That's all gone through,' the alluring presence confirmed, casting a beguiling smile at this potential adversary. She held Cat's eyes with an intense gaze, attempting to establish what made her tick.

Cat, unaware of this hidden agenda, voiced her approval of this unexpected, excellent service. 'Thank you so much for all your help.'

'No problem, come again.'

'I most certainly will,' Cat enthused. And as she turned to leave ...

'Just a sec, Cat. Let me take a guess ... I bet you're a nurse.'

'Goodness. How did you work that out?'

'Oh, I dunno. I seem to have a knack for it.'

'Amazing! Well, bye for now, and thanks for your help.'

Kayleigh found herself looking forward to the next meeting when a clearer understanding of this redhead would help her formulate her chosen plan.

Cat jumped back into the Zoe, relieved to see that Spot and Roxy were not covered in blood.

'God, that woman was so helpful, she just seems too good to be true,' Cat said.

'Yeah, my friend has been in there a few times. She said that nothing seemed to be too much trouble. What was her name again, Kerry, or something?'

Cat corrected her: 'Kayleigh.'

I knew it! Spot thought. *Kayleigh—my nemesis has come back to haunt me. Cat ought to be careful.*

Cat dropped Roxy off at her flat, thanking her profusely for her help and support with Spot. Naturally, they gave each other a light embrace, which quickly escalated.

'Roxy,' Cat said, coming up for air, 'I'll never take for granted what we have. Don't ever allow this to stop.'

Roxy replied, eyes sparkling, silently vowing to never cease worshipping her newfound hero. 'No way Cat!'

'Same again tomorrow?' Cat suggested, smiling at Roxy mischievously. Roxy returned her reply.

Of course, they both knew it wouldn't be that easy —who could know what the future might hold? Despite sensing that things might never be quite the same again, Cat was determined to keep this delicious affaire de cœur alive.

Roxy, opening her door, suddenly called back, 'Oh, by the way, when you were in the shop, Spot seemed a bit agitated.'

'Hmm ... I guess it'll take time before he's comfortable with his new situation.'

'I'm sure you're right.'

Cat let out a breath: 'Come on then, Spot! It's just you and me, for now.'

Cat and Spot were passing through the gate to the backyard when Cat realised it must be toilet time for Spot.

I thought you would never ask, Spot thought, immediately trotting off to find a more private place to relieve himself. Cat scooped up the poo with a piece of kitchen roll, thinking, Oh, the joys of dog ownership!

'Come on, Spot! Let's go in and discover what the efficient shopkeeper has given you in your doggy bag.'

Cat emptied the contents onto her kitchen work surface, pleasantly surprised at the useful canine-related assortment. She filled up Spot's new water bowl and placed it down for the grateful Jack Russell.

Now for his first meal, Doggy Delight. In seconds, Spot devoured this doggy yum-yum; the bowl emptied with absolutely no traces of food left. Spot looked up expectantly at Cat as if to say, *Come on then, what about afters: Irresistible to Dogs biscuits?*

Cat duly refilled the bowl, whereupon Spot consumed, less rapidly, roughly half the contents.

'Okay, I think I'm getting it now,' Cat concluded.

Spot looked into Cat's face as if to confirm this sentiment.

'Good boy, Spot!'

Cat put the kettle on and made a light snack. She didn't normally eat a massive amount at home. The sponsored hospital cuisine was both good value and nutritious, so why bother cooking, except for special occasions?

Her thoughts strayed to her new pal, Roxette. I'll invite her to dinner one night, without going over the top. Cat's willpower was strong enough to ensure her trim figure remained intact, and she intended to keep it that way. She was sure Roxy felt the same about preserving her gorgeous body. Just thinking about her aroused Cat. *Careful, baby!*

Spot settled under the kitchen table on his old bed— another donation from Mrs Nosey Parker.

He was thinking about the shop when Cat announced, 'I'll take you out onto the canal in an hour or so Spot. We need to give your grub a chance to go down.'

With that, Spot settled down, feeling apprehensive but looking forward to another nap and another proper walk.

Where will she take me—a canal—the canal? What are the chances of that? And what if Kayleigh's there? Jeepers creepers!

He shut his little eyes, and despite his worries, he had a good feeling about this new owner. She seemed to understand canines.

Spot drifted off, defiantly confident that he could deal with anything anyone threw at him—and then some! Welcome to the new Spot, sponsored by Cat. She genuinely appeared to care about him. Care? Hmm ... considering the Nosey Parkers and all the others, he concluded that care is a very unusual trait in humans.

Having finished her remaining chores, Cat fished out the basic dog lead thoughtfully provided by the shopkeeper and went into the kitchen to Spot's basket. It was empty!

'Oh my God, I've lost him before I've even started!' But as she turned, there was Spot, standing in the doorway wagging his tiny tail in eager anticipation of a walk.

‘Spot! You frightened me!’ Cat exclaimed, pretending to scold him. But Spot knew there was no malice there.

She leaned down to attach the lead to Spot’s collar, pulled her coat on, slipped into her new wellies, checked she had her keys and phone, and they were through the front door. Cat noted it was not raining now but acknowledged that this might not always be the case. She was adamant they would not be simply fair-weather walkers, like so many of the ‘city’ types around here, so she’d purchase wet weather gear for both of them at the first opportunity.

The sky was still light as the canal came into view. Lush parkland leading up to the hospital flanked the water. Then, the towpath narrowed and continued alongside trees and hedges lining the canal. They padded on in the failing light; the walk becoming less appealing.

‘Hmm,’ Cat muttered to Spot, ‘I’m not sure we would want to be out here on a dark night.’

Spot glanced up at his companion, his expression suggesting agreement. Of course, he had elemental experience in the perhaps-to-be-repeated scenario. This, he now attempted to convey telepathically to Cat.

Taking it in, only up to a point, Cat noted the fast-approaching dusk, which prompted an immediate about turn and a brisk return home. They trooped into the backyard as the evening gloom descended.

'Not a bad start for both of us, eh, Fella?' Cat said, congratulating their achievement. She unlocked the back door, took off her wellies and stepped in. Turning to Spot, she said, 'Wait there, Spot. I need to run some warm, soapy water in a bucket to wash the mud off your paws and my foot gear, okay?' Spot obeyed.

Cat returned with the necessary equipment, giving the offending paws and her apparel a cursory douse. Then, after drying Spot and herself off with an old but effective towel, she followed Spot inside.

With Spot content on his bed, chewing a treat, Cat snuggled up on the settee, her own liquid treat by her side on the accessible, very occasional table. She reflected warmly on the last few days. In no time, she had transformed her lonely house into a loving home. Not only had she successfully acquired a new doggy companion, but she had also met up with an extremely beautiful, valued new friend and colleague—Roxette. She felt truly blessed.

Rather less enthusiastically, Cat's thoughts turned to the shopkeeper, who had been unusually keen to go the extra mile to help a total stranger.

A steely Cat grabbed her glass, banged it down on the sink and checked on Spot. He seemed fine. She made a point of setting the wake-up alarm an hour earlier than usual. She was working the next day, so she'd need extra time to take

Spot out for their brief walk. Settling her head onto the pillow, a contented Cat was out, in an instant.

The Being decided its plan may need certain adjustments to accommodate the astute workings of the red-haired beauty's mind. Again, it was becoming abundantly clear that she would not be the pushover that the Being preferred.

Chapter 14

The Being: Not Happy

'Come on Luv, for God's sake! I ain't got all day!' an unkempt, overweight man yelled as he pushed past the browsing customers to join the end of the queue in the corner shop.

The other customers—patiently waiting—turned, curious to see who owned the rude voice. They stared at him. Unruffled, Kayleigh carried on serving at her usual efficient pace.

He'd been in before, behaving in a similarly boorish manner—loudly threatening to go to Abdul's Emporium, up the road, where the 'service was better'. But then, he couldn't stand the smell of curry! Kayleigh ignored him, not interested in who he was, inwardly referring to him as the Aberration.

'Look 'ere! I'm a decent electrician, I haven't got time for this. I've got an appointment in ten minutes. If I'm not there, I could lose the job, and the customer would lose the benefit of my great work'—as if it was their problem, not his, for being late. With that attitude, no one would want him digging in their garden, let alone working in their house. One man decided action was required. He exited the queue and shuffled up to the 'problem'.

'Look here, Pal! You've got two choices,' he asserted, pushing his face directly into the offender's outstandingly ugly mush. 'One, wait in line like the rest of us or get the fuck out of here. What's it to be?'

The electrician backed off. 'Okay, okay, I'll wait.'

'One more word, and I'll smash that stupid face in. Got it?'

'S-sure, mate. Got it!' Like most bullies, the suddenly anxious electrician couldn't 'take it' himself. He shut up.

Kayleigh smiled sardonically as she motioned the next customer forward. An elderly, frail customer approached, commenting, 'There's always one, dear, isn't there?'

Kayleigh, smiling her a knowing look, stifled a desire to state out loud that she hoped there would be one less in due course—she'd rather not have a heart attack on her hands in the shop.

'Five cans of Doggy Delight, please.' Kayleigh instantly produced the requested best seller.

'Ooh! Thank you so much,' the salt of the earth declared, the successful purchase making her day. Her adorable pooch: mad for it.

This is what it was all about for Kayleigh. *Did she still have a heart?* While she was debating this, the electrician appeared in front of her. And when he started his garrulous monotones, as he'd done in the past, the Being inside her took centre stage. *Heart? Maybe not.*

'Oh!' the electrician exclaimed, 'I could have had that effing plumber. Just wait till next time.'

Kayleigh, barely perceptibly, shook her head, unable to believe what she was hearing.

'Anyhow,' he said, 'I'm going for a jog the day after tomorrow—when this crap weather is supposed to be drying up.'

The other customers sighed noisily, wondering how long this tedious conversation would continue. But Kayleigh carried on regardless. She couldn't stop now.

'Really?' patronised Kayleigh, leading him on, which wasn't difficult. 'Where do you usually go?'

'On the canal. I usually get as far as where it narrows to the trees and bushes.'

‘Oh! I would look out for yourself. Who knows what might happen?’

‘Oh, yeah, no problem.’

Really? reflected the internal Being with previous.

‘Do you normally meet anyone there?’ Kayleigh quizzed, wondering who in their right mind would want him for company.

‘Well, I’d love to see you there, babe!’ replied the electrician, his twisted mind taking this as an invitation, which, of course, it was.

You can count on it! The voice in her head promised calmly.

Kayleigh couldn’t resist giving him one more bit of rope to hang himself. ‘About what time will you be there?

‘Oh, at about eight.’ The Being made a mental note.

The cursed electrician turned and departed the scene, calling out, ‘See ya later!’

Kayleigh silently credited him with a backhanded compliment for being so unknowingly prescient. ‘Yep, see you later!’ Kayleigh affirmed, barely able to breathe, excitement welling up at the prospect of her upcoming fulfilment.

The patient queue of customers looked at one another, rolled their eyes heavenward and breathed a collective sigh of relief to see the back of him at last.

Next up was the hero, who had confronted the difficulty. Kayleigh was not too sure about him. Seán, the local plumber, and local gossip had it that he was a serial womaniser. Those blue eyes, she knew only too well from her own experience, probably enabled him to get away with murder. His wife having just given birth, found out that he had the gall to start an affair with the local sub-post mistress—on their proverbial doorstep! Unbelievably, he still got away with it. The smiling philanderer looked directly into Kayleigh's eyes, stating with practised charm,

'Hello, Kayleigh, you look fabulous today.' He had a slight sniffle, but that wouldn't stop him.

'Hello, Casanova, to what do we owe the pleasure?' she replied, returning a perfunctory smile while noting those enticing blue eyes. Irrationally, Kayleigh found herself secretly pleased with the flattering compliment. Casanova's gaze plunged, drinking in the shopkeeper's trim body.

She could feel him undressing her. And she enjoyed the attention. *What the hell? Why shouldn't I?* she thought. The exhibitionist inside her reaping the rewards of her unconscious efforts.

'I'm going for a bike ride by the canal, and I need a puncture repair kit, please, my love,' Casanova requested in a smooth, measured tone, his gaze not leaving Kayleigh's mesmerised face.

On hearing the word canal, Kayleigh instantly came to her senses. The fledgling romantic spell was well and truly broken, temporarily at least. *Hmm … this new information could be useful,* she thought.

Reverting to the job at hand, she set the kit on the counter. He paid her in cash—he was a dodgy plumber, after all. Kayleigh's mind went into overdrive. She had to think quickly.

As he turned to go … *ah-ah-atishoo!* Fumbling for a tissue, he blew his nose noisily.

'That sounds like a nasty cold,' observed Kayleigh.

Sniff. 'It's not too bad.' *Sniff.* 'Have a good day, Kayleigh,' he replied, attempting to retrieve the situation. Too late. It was becoming clear to him that other forces were at work here. He knew when to back off.

On his way out, he inadvertently dropped his tissue. Kayleigh sidled out from behind the counter. She politely asked the next punter to please bear with her, as she leant down to retrieve the potential 'Exhibit A'. Kayleigh bagged it, being careful not to touch it with her fingers, dog owner style.

'Yes! I have a plan.' Kayleigh felt the elation building inside her. She concealed the crucial bag where she was sure no one would find it.

The next customer, perplexed, inquired, 'Err . . . have you found what you were looking for?'

'Oh yes, thanks,' Kayleigh replied self-consciously. 'And now, what can I get you?' she asked, back behind the counter, reverting to her role as servant to the proles.

She smiled in satisfaction at the thought of her plan, hastily concocted under pressure. She also acknowledged the charisma the plumber had brazenly paraded in front of her, even when not one hundred percent fit.

Chapter 15

Dawn

In the corner shop the next day, Kayleigh slipped into autopilot. Her parents had spent years doing what their daughter had only been doing for weeks. But Kayleigh had already twigged how familiarity could easily breed contempt, especially given the customers she had to deal with. Fortunately, that dickhead the electrician, was a rarity. The majority were pleasant and helped to pass the time of day agreeably.

'Thank you, Peter,' Kayleigh said appreciatively. Peter beamed with satisfaction.

As she waited for the next customer to step up, Kayleigh glanced across to the shop entrance for a change of scenery, if nothing else. A feeling of disbelief matched her face as a new customer stepped in. Kayleigh only had a vague recollection of who it was. If memory served, she had been in once before, just after the shop had reopened.

'What was her name?' she asked herself. 'Got it! Dawn, the electrician's wife!' *How weird is that?*

Dawn had forgotten a couple of things in her weekly big shop, and she had also heard that the corner shop had improved dramatically. The shopkeeper was in attendance for a change, at least.

Kayleigh waited while the newly returning customer made her way over to the counter. A sudden instinct came into Kayleigh's head. She was not a hundred percent sure that her plan to deflect the blame for what she was about to carry out was completely watertight. She needed a backup—Plan B! On seeing Dawn, Kayleigh sensed that Plan B might be about to present itself.

'Can I help you? It's Dawn Jacques, isn't it?' Kayleigh purred to the startled young woman.

'Why, yes!' Dawn replied. 'Well-remembered!' She glanced around, 'Golly, it looks like you have everything here.'

'Well, we do try.' Kayleigh said, gesturing over to her assistant Connie, who duly smiled back. Kayleigh's well-honed instinct kicked in as she weighed up this potential pawn in her deadly game.

'But do you have Turkish delight chunks in a box and pear cider?' asked Dawn, testing the shopkeeper, teasingly.

'How many would you like of each?' Kayleigh countered triumphantly.

'Wow! Now I am impressed,' Dawn had to concede.

The shop was quiet for a change, so Kayleigh, having started the softening-up process, continued to chat with Dawn. She needed to extract as much information as possible to work out her rapidly developing plan.

'And how is your husband? I'm sorry; what's his name again?' Kayleigh asked.

'Gary. But to be honest,' she said, lowering her voice, 'we haven't been getting along too well just lately.' Dawn's heart was sinking fast.

Kayleigh's plan was working. The number of customers who wanted to spill their hearts out to hairdressers or shopkeepers, ready to trust them implicitly, never ceased to amaze her.

'In what way?' enquired the 'therapist' Kayleigh.

Dawn carried on, thinking that this was indeed a therapy session, but more beneficial and without the professional waiting to trip her up. Unknown to her, however, the local gossip had entered the establishment. What the gossip didn't know wasn't worth knowing. She made a business out of it. Dawn rambled on, relieved at last to have a sympathetic shoulder to cry on.

‘Oh! His past misdemeanours I used to be able to forget; we were inseparable at one time. But what he’s been up to lately—well, I just don’t know anymore.’ Dawn broke down.

Kayleigh came from behind the counter to comfort the distressed young woman. Dawn looked into her new confidante’s face, declaring, ‘I just want him out of my life now.’

The village gossip beamed from ear to ear.

Kayleigh was her own fiercest critic. She considered her performance—not bad so far. However, there was one last detail to sort out.

Dawn gestured for Kayleigh to come closer. ‘God knows why I’m telling you this,’ she whispered, ‘but I really need to talk to him face to face. I want a divorce. I’m on antidepressants. My job in the ICU is getting to me, and I just can’t sleep anymore.’

Kayleigh’s brain was on red alert. *ICU? The ICU where Declan was? The ICU where Cat works?* Pulling herself back and sensing she was getting somewhere, Kayleigh whispered, ‘Did you know Gary was in my shop yesterday? If you’re sure you want to act . . . he said he was going jogging along the canal tomorrow at about 8.30 pm.’

Dawn grasped at what she thought was this heaven-sent opportunity to finally get shot of him. She could make it happen. ‘Really? I’ll be there!’ she replied. She felt good.

Oh, so good.

Kayleigh was pleased with Plan B.

The village gossip, although having struggled to hear the last part of the conversation, was also pleased with the intriguing snippets of info she'd gleaned. Especially the part where the woman said that she 'just wanted him out of her life now.'

'Someone is going to be interested in that,' she muttered. The village gossip, with all her years of experience, just knew.

The Being, Kayleigh, lurked amongst the trees and bushes beyond the parkland on the now isolated canal. Dusk was falling and flecks of drizzle fell from the gloomy evening sky. A jogger—well, more of a less-than-expedient pedestrian—padded along the towpath in Kayleigh's direction.

'Phew! It's alright for you!' he complained to a disinterested duck. 'Sod this for a game of soldiers! After the twats that I have to deal with, surely I deserve more than this.' The duck swam on, oblivious to his plight.

Puffing and gasping, the exhausted jogger collapsed in a sorry heap onto a convenient bench near where Kayleigh was hiding. Talk about tempting fate. Kayleigh moved in; gloves on, kitchen knife poised.

Using parlance he would readily understand, she spat, 'This is for all the shit you've dished out to so many. Prepare to meet your maker!'

'Kayleigh, is that you? What the, who the . . . ?'

The apology for a human was in shock, motionless. He couldn't begin to predict what was about to happen. But he'd find out, in the flash of a knife.

With surprising strength and dexterity, the petite entity grabbed his wiry hair, wrenched her victim's head back with one hand and with the other, slashed his gross neck from ear to ear, the ten-inch, razor-sharp domestic implement causing fountains of blood to gush everywhere. With devilish strength, she shoved the rapidly expiring electrician into his watery resting place. *Splash!*

Her trademark execution, complete.

An overwhelming satisfaction engulfed her. In Kayleigh's mind, she'd efficiently eliminated another useless piece of shit.

Now, to tidy up the murder scene. Acting quickly, and continuously checking for hapless walkers, she filled her blood-stained gloves with stones and dumped them into the murky waters. She didn't want her DNA on the next task she was about to perform. Yanking a clean pair of gloves from her pocket, she pulled out the plastic bag containing the plumber's snotty tissue. She rubbed the contaminated tissue over the handle to ensure the transference of the unethical philanderer's DNA. All that remained was to get rid of the plastic bag, the tissue, and her blood-splattered coat. She shoved the bag and the tissue into her coat, and after filling the pockets with more stones, adios-ed the lot into the canal.

She shuffled into the bushes and absently dropped the murder weapon, intending the police to find it. They would examine it, note the traces of the plumber's DNA, and find him guilty of the murder.

She looked around again, and ensuring there were no witnesses, sent the second pair of gloves to join the other evidence in the canal.

Instinctively, Kayleigh looked back down the canal. *Uh-oh!* A slightly built figure was staggering towards her. She just knew it was Dawn. Kayleigh's cunning brain whirred into action as a modified Plan B flashed before her.

'Yes, Got it!'

Retrieving the discarded knife, she cleaned it swiftly. She placed it onto the towpath, where Dawn couldn't possibly miss it. That done, she retreated behind a tree to monitor the upcoming events.

Sure enough, Dawn approached, and noticing an unexpected knife lying on the path, picked it up. She passed it from hand to hand, wondering, *What the heck is a kitchen knife doing on a canal towpath?* But then she thought that maybe a canal boat owner had mislaid it. *They're sure to be back for it soon.* So she dropped it where she had found it.

‘I really need to get home. Which way is it?’ She turned; her mind upside down, thinking, *This must be the way.* Fortunately for her, it was.

An ecstatic Kayleigh watched Dawn pass out of sight. She headed home on cloud nine, knowing that victory was now assured.

Back at the corner shop, her feet still not touching the ground, she congratulated herself on a job well done. But then, her thoughts returned to the other significant development that had recently transpired in the shop—the meeting with the plumber.

Kayleigh reviewed her position. The police would find Dawn guilty of the murder and the plumber would be reprieved. She had made sure of that. Satisfied, she allowed herself a period of luxuriant reflection.

Chapter 16

Nature or Nurture

A dog had escaped from its new home via the back gate, instinctively wanting to discover or mark its fresh territory. That's what dogs do. Cat had let Spot out of the back door for a pee, failing to notice that the gate was not completely shut.

Spot trotted across the road and headed for the canal. There were sure to be plenty of doggy smells there. Having crossed the park, he arrived.

A jogger appeared, staggering, looking decidedly worse for wear. Spot carried on for a bit, only hesitating to pick up the unmistakable scent of a rabbit. But as it was getting late, he headed back down the canal to his comfortable new home and cosy bed.

Suddenly, a blood-curdling scream pierced the night air, ceasing abruptly. Spot was transfixed. A resounding splash jolted him back to life.

Looking back, frightened at what he might witness, he saw a shimmering, silvery-grey, ephemeral apparition push a hefty body into the canal with what looked like supernatural strength. The Being turned. It had sensed someone, or something, was watching. It recognised the dog, its adversary of old.

Spot, likewise, knew at once it was Kayleigh. His visceral instincts kicked in. He turned tail and ran away as fast as he could, imagining the Being chasing him. He looked back. The jogger had gone. But he thought he heard voices coming from the direction of the bridge.

The disquieting incident almost overwhelmed him.

When he thought it was safe, Spot slowed down to look behind. Seeing no one, he paused and jumped behind a large tree, peeping out to make doubly sure it didn't pursue him. *Whew!* He was shaking from head to tail, breathing in great gasps of air as his rattled body gradually recovered.

A sudden, strong feeling of déjà vu engulfed him. *My God, the Being is back—Kayleigh!*

Come on Spot, son! Get a grip! He felt a rush of guilt for unnecessarily upsetting his new friend. *I need to get home; she'll be panicking. I need to protect her.*

Warily, he backtracked, his eyes scanning all around, a feeling of extreme trepidation pervading. He reached the fight scene where a pool of blood had trickled from the tow-path bank into the water. There was no one to be seen, thank God. Quickly now, he ran for home, finally crashing through the back gate and up to the back door, which was unexpectedly shut.

He let out a series of agitated barks. The door flung open. Cat stood there in her coat, aghast with grief.

'Spot! Where the hell have you been? I've been worried sick!' Cat blurted out. 'I was just about to go out and look for you!'

Spot's ears went back in a heartfelt apology.

'Come on in!' Cat instructed. 'I'll get you some food. You look terrible.'

It was way past bedtime when Spot finally settled onto his bed. This time Cat made doubly sure all the doors and the back gate were shut and locked.

The following morning, she would take Spot out for a walk. Yet, as she got ready for bed, she had a niggling feeling that something unexpected was in the air. She shut her eyes, weird dreams now accompanying her fitful sleep.

Dawn arrived at the park near the canal towpath at the time suggested by that wonderful shopkeeper. She waited restlessly for her unthinkable apology of a husband, hopefully soon to be her ex.

Earlier that evening, two lads were strolling along the towpath, with their snooker cue containers under their arms, looking forward to a game of pool. A sudden loud splash stopped them in their tracks. 'Wow, Tyrone; up ahead. Did you see that?' Jerome cried.

'What the . . . ? Someone's standing on the bank looking into the water. God!'

'Yet another piss-up, gone massively wrong, I reckon.' Jerome knew a thing or two about piss-ups.

'Oh well! There's not much we can do. Better not get involved. Come on, let's get out of here! Snooker awaits!' The twins loved their pool.

The lads arrived at the snooker club only to find it was shut, 'due to refurbishment.'

'Oh, no, Tyrone! Would you effing believe it?'

'I guess we'll have to take it out on those more-ish Munster cans in front of another dose of Netflix on the widescreen.' Jerome reflected.

'Yeah, guess so,' his twin grudgingly agreed.

On reaching the park, they noticed a confused-looking woman wandering around aimlessly.

‘Are you alright, love?’ the upstanding citizen enquired of the slightly built woman. Tyrone thought that he’d seen her before. Of course! The splash that they had witnessed on the way here.

‘Uh! Alright? What? N-not really,’ she muttered.

‘Where do you live, missus? We’ll take you home,’ the samaritans graciously offered.

‘Err . . . Smith Street.’

‘That’s just across the way from us,’ Jerome said. ‘Come on then. Let’s get you home.’

While they walked, Tyrone looked across at the woman, thinking, something strange was going down. They located her house after a few false starts and safely deposited the waif indoors.

‘Are you going to be okay? Is there anyone in to look after you?’ Tyrone asked.

‘I th-think so,’ was the unsure answer. ‘But don’t worry, and thank you for your help,’ she said, hastily shutting the door. Dawn, comprehensively appalled at her recent discovery of her husband’s repulsive ‘activities’, could not care less where he stayed for the night, as long as he didn’t show up at the now-defiled marital home.

And that was it.

The lads looked at each other, and concluding that at least they had got her home, they resumed their laddish life, as lads do.

The plumber unlocked his shed door and pulled out his trusty steed. He hadn't got much on today, although unscheduled emergencies were always a possibility. But as he had promised himself an early morning ride, he was gonna go for it. It had rained during the night. He had his all-weather kit on, so he wasn't much bothered about the conditions.

Passing the hospital, he rode through the park and headed onto the canal. The towpath was muddy, and as he squelched and slid along, both he and his bike soon got thoroughly plastered. After a couple of miles and realising this was becoming a bit of a pain, he stopped by a bench for a rest and a few sips from his plastic drinking bottle. As he recovered his breath, he could feel his phone vibrating in his inside pocket.

'Uh-oh! I thought it was too good to be true.'

'Hi Seán, this is Letitia from Mount Pleasant. Sorry to bother you so early, but I can smell gas by my boiler and I'm a bit worried about it. How are you fixed?'

'Oh, okay, Letitia. I'm just out on my bike, but I will get to you as soon as I get back. Now, listen! This is important. Turn off the gas at the meter and open all the windows. Can you do that?'

'Hang on . . . just a sec . . . I think I've done it!' the lovely Letitia gushed.

'Great! Now turn your cooker on to make sure there's no gas coming through,' Seán advised calmly.

'Yeah! Nothing's coming out.'

'Good, well done! Don't turn any lights on or use any electrical items. I'll see you shortly.'

'Thank you, Seán,' came the grateful reply.

Jesus H Christ, he said to himself as he got back on his bike and headed back down the towpath.

Concentrating on the terrain in front of him, he asked himself, *Was that the remains of blood on the ground back there? There was a lot of it.*

He got off his bike and walked back to the spillage, noting a narrow tyre track passing right through it, which he presumed was his own, going out. Shrugging his shoulders, he got back on his bike. *I've got to get to Mount Pleasant and prevent a potential gas explosion. I haven't got time to play amateur detective.* But just as he was about to get back on his bike, his phone rang again.

'Seán! Hi! It's Melanie from Moseley. I've just got back from work and there is an inch of water all over the kitchen floor. Help!'

Seán quickly explained his need to attend to an emergency gas leak but would get around as soon as possible. The lovely Melanie trusted her hero.

'Okay, see you soon.'

And with that, he cracked on, his mind now turning to the supposed gas leak. He'd seen it all before, of course. It might be a genuine emergency, or the cat might have just peed up the corner—the smell being similar. Who knows? What he did know was that it was, historically, always a joyful experience with Letitia.

Cat sipped her last drop of coffee, replacing the mug on the coaster.

'Come on then, Spot! Time for walkies.'

Spot was on it, lead in mouth, raring to go.

Faraway *nee-naw, nee-naw* sounds suddenly filled the air, rapidly intensifying into a crescendo. Cat pulled the curtain back just enough to see emergency vehicles racing past the end of the road.

Blue lights swirled across the park, heading for the canal. Spot appeared at Cat's side, glancing up at her face as if to say, there's going to be trouble. Cat took this on board.

'Looks like our walk will have to wait, Spot. God knows what's going on there, but we don't want to get mixed up in it, do we? Let's just see what it was all about when I get back tonight.'

He whimpered his agreement. Cat let him out into the backyard to do his business. Spot would have the rest of the day to work it all out. He had half of the story, of course, but as for the rest, *who knows?*

Cat left for work, voicing her apologies to Spot.

No probs, he thought. But as he settled into his bed, his eyes were sad. In the short time they had been together, a bond had formed, almost telepathic. His thoughts turned back to the canal and the sensational return of the Being that was Kayleigh. He felt a shiver. *Come on Spot, you know you can stand up to her,* he reminded himself. He needed that telepathy with Cat to work now. He had to make her aware that Kayleigh was back, and they'd need to deal with her accordingly. Spot knew this was probably easier said than done, but he had to find a way of communicating this to Cat as soon as possible. And he couldn't forget the man's scent on her.

Cat set off with the sound of sirens still in her ears.

'Flip me!' she said. 'It never rains, but it pours.'

Chapter 17

An Impossible Schedule

In the ICU, a tired-looking nurse announced to the rest of the team her intention to clock off: the twelve-hour shift taking its toll. Dawn was freshening up in the washroom when her phone rang, somewhere in her clothes. She couldn't be arsed to hunt for it, knowing it would go to answerphone before she could find it. She made her way to her Shangri-La; the canteen. The exhausted nurse was hungry.

'Yes, love, what can I get you?'

'Oh! A toasted tea cake and a cup of tea, please.' Dawn waged a constant war on her calorie count, like most people. Unlike most people, she'd got it under control. The petite, slim nurse picked her tray up, and imparting her thanks, trudged to an empty table.

Suddenly remembering the unanswered phone call, Dawn belatedly fished her phone out of her pocket, thinking, who the heck could that have been? She didn't recognise the number, but the caller had left a voice message.

Hello, Mrs Jacques, this is West Midlands Police. It's important that you please call us as soon as possible. The caller read out the contact number.

The stunned nurse sat there thinking; *Whoa! What can that be about, and where did they get my number from? Is it something to do with my pathetic, estranged husband? God knows what he's been up to.*

A switch flicked in her mind—the unwelcome memories flooding back into her subconscious. She felt a wave of panic.

Imagining all sorts of scenarios and coming to no conclusions, an increasingly physically and emotionally shattered woman decided to go home. She had no strength to deal with this additional problem until the morning.

One last corner to go. Turning it, Dawn gasped. She saw a police car parked outside her flat. With her strength ebbing away, she staggered past the striped car, noting there were two officers inside. Gingerly, she approached her front door, fiddling and failing to get her key into the lock. Inwardly cursing her estranged waste-of-time husband for the thousandth time, she thought, *Christ, if this is him, what kind of trouble has that bastard got me into now?*

Flashbacks of all of his past indiscretions overwhelmed her.

'Are you alright, madam?' inquired the approaching WPC.

Startled, Dawn, remembering the scene at the canal, panicked and made to run away. But the metal mud scraper by the door caught her foot. Over she went, headfirst, her forehead striking the unforgiving concrete slabs. Blood gushed from the deep gash, the pain now starting. And with that, she fainted, her body deciding enough is enough.

'Bloody Nora! How did that happen?' the stunned PC asked his partner.

'Christ knows!' his equally non-plussed colleague replied, shaking her head.

The officers sprang into action, summoning the ambulance service immediately. In the meantime, they attended to the lady as best they could—only too aware of the potential consequences of a blow to the head.

As they waited, the bemused officers considered their conundrum. The original intention was to gain access to the home of the murder victim's wife and assess the situation regarding the lady's mental wellbeing. If it were appropriate, they would, as compassionately as possible, inform her of the demise of her husband. The other important task was to assess the chances of Mrs Jacques potentially being implicated in her husband's murder. But that had all gone out of the window, considering the lady's attempted escape and the mental state she appeared to be in. And now, the injury to her head added further complications.

'We're a bit out of our depth here,' WPC Smith conceded. 'We need to talk to the gaffer.'

Her colleague agreed, getting into the car and onto the blower. Taking in HQ's advice, he replaced the handset.

'They're going to contact the hospital to tell them what has happened,' he explained to his partner. 'They'll send high-ranking officers to meet up with the doctors to map out a way forward. We're to follow on to the hospital to observe Mrs Jacques—she's a potential murder suspect, after all.'

WPC Smith nodded her assent.

The cops breathed sighs of relief and followed the ambulance to the hospital.

At the hospital, the porters pushed the groggy, bandaged woman through the ward doors and over to the nurse to assess her.

'It's Dawn Jacques!' the shocked nurse cried, rushing over to the trolley. 'Look at her head! Whatever's happened to her?'

Three off-duty nurses surrounded their beleaguered colleague's bed. The Police Officers stood at a discreet distance and let the professionals get on with their jobs.

'Dawn definitely looked knackered last night, but what the heck?' a concerned staff member puzzled.

Dawn finally opened her eyes, expecting her cat, Fluffy, would be on the end of the bed.

'Fluffy! Where are you?'

A nurse leant down to her. 'Dawn, love, you've had a bit of a fall, but you are with your friends in the hospital. Everything's going to be alright.'

Recognising a colleague, a mightily relieved Dawn felt the weight of the world might finally lift off her shoulders. The nurse offered her medication and a glass of water.

'Here, Dawn, take these!'

'Oh, thank you,' she breathed. Shutting her eyes again, Dawn drifted off to a desperately needed sleep, surrounded by her mystified colleagues.

Witnessing the scene, two senior doctors metaphorically scratched their respective chins, thinking, *What's happening here?*

The cops also added their incomprehension, thinking, with their trained instinct, supposedly to the fore; *She looks as guilty as hell.* They fleetingly reflected on the similarities between the murder of Mr Jacques and the 'bodies in the canal' case. And then they reminded each other of the unsolved double murders of Shannon and Ronan: Declan's next-door neighbours. Not done in at the canal but by the same modus operandi.

Having discounted the hospitalised Declan, the police investigation into Mr Jacques' murder began in the shop. Kayleigh provided details of those who were present at the same time as Dawn was there; cunningly omitting the intimate details they had shared. In contrast, the village gossip relished recounting the conversation she'd overheard.

The senior officers' interrogation of Seán was intense, giving him the third degree. The DNA from the victim's blood, splattered all over his mountain bike, was a rich source of evidence. They kept him in custody for the customary twenty-four hours, pending further evidence. This evidence was slow in coming.

The detective chief inspector and detective sergeant knew if they failed to find enough evidence to convict Seán, they'd have to release him after twenty-four hours. They needed more time. The superintendent obligingly granted an extension to hold him for thirty-six hours. In the event, his DNA proved only that he had been at the scene. What they needed was the murder weapon. The plumber's solicitor knew only too well that. Although inconclusive, this DNA evidence could be enough to find his client guilty in the absence of stronger evidence from another source. Next, it was the snooker lads' turn. Not much to go on there. They weren't sure that the wandering lady they had taken home was the figure they saw shoving someone into the canal.

The police eventually found the knife. The DNA proved to be Dawn's. When the police questioned her in the hospital, the officer asked her straight out, 'Mrs Jacques, are you responsible for murdering your husband?'

'I—I'm sorry. I'm really not sure. I could be, I suppose. I just can't remember.'

After all the evidence was in, the verdict was inevitable: Dawn was found guilty.

All of Dawn's friends, colleagues, and acquaintances gathered around her hospital bed. All of them thought they should have recognised the anguish she was going through and why they didn't do something about it.

However, despite her guilty verdict, she was released into secure accommodation on the grounds of diminished responsibility.

Dawn experienced a rush of optimism. 'If I've really killed him, then all of this pain has been worth it. Now I can look forward to a wonderful life in care, without the unwanted negatives of that 'Unthinkable'. Good riddance. He's finally gone where he belongs.'

The plumber, on the other hand, was in a proper two-and-eight: losing sleep, hardly able to eat, wondering if they'd bring him back into custody. He was unaware that Dawn had been accused on the grounds of diminished responsibility. When the wheels of justice caught up with real-time, he was informed that he was absolved of any blame, his record, clean.

He was, of course, mightily relieved at his good fortune, but had to express to his solicitor his disgust in the legal system.

'Now look 'ere. What kind of justice is this if an innocent person, in the wrong place at the wrong time, could be compelled to rely on a 'lucky escape' to have his name cleared? Tell me that!'

The solicitor simply shrugged his shoulders. 'Welcome to the system!' he said. 'I've seen and heard it all before.'

The working-class hero simply reverted to type, opinionated, 'Well, don't take this personally, but the system stinks,' he said.

The apologetic solicitor had to agree, 'Yes, sometimes it does!'

Kayleigh sat alone, her admirable assistant, Connie and the punters, gone—the shop eerily quiet, a cup of coffee her only companion. A massive sense of anti-climax swept over her.

She needed to take stock.

She reflected on her troubled upbringing. Her 'parents', perennially absent, a lonely child, passed from pillar to post, plucking at straws, attempting to make some sense of her young life, single-handily. Among the many negatives, two events remained locked away in her subconscious that could not be accessed easily. One was self-inflicted, the other inflicted upon her. Either had the potential to destroy the balance of her mind, so that was where they would stay—in her mind. This was the only way she could cope. And it worked.

Kayleigh knew she was different, resulting from all the negatives thrown at her throughout her life. Potential friends were quickly dispensed with—unknown motives suspected. Always a loner—now the finished article.

If a fly dared to come too near, she would instantly exterminate it; it was a threat. Kill, or be killed, was the mantra immediately leaping to the fore, eclipsing anything else. Kayleigh connected to that atavistic era. She totally bought into the concept, sensing that she was inescapably a throwback to that historically turbulent time.

And was that merely a convenient excuse? Kayleigh concluded, unequivocally, that it was. Kayleigh had long ago come to terms with the situation when the Being part of her dominated, relishing the powers available to her.

Kayleigh had gone through the motions of being a dutiful wife to her boring husband. That had ultimately failed miserably. Then a brief fling with Declan, which also ended disastrously. But Kayleigh needed to move on.

'That young woman sleeping with Cat—hmm— Roxy, is it?'

When Roxy next appeared in her shop, Kayleigh decided she'd look deeply into her stellar eyes. She would look for any reaction to her subtle powers of seduction to see where they might lead. If there would be strings attached, then it would be a strict no-no. Kayleigh did not do strings.

Kayleigh's thoughts turned to the philanderer she'd chosen to save. The Plumber, or Casanova as she referred to him, also had mileage. *There will not be any such commitment issues in his case, that's for sure. For Christ's sake, given his reputation, I have the distinct feeling he doesn't do strings either! Perfect!*

Cat might not be happy about the Being's imminent pursuit of her lover, but the troubled, emotional mess that was Kayleigh, felt life owed her these tiny chinks of pleasure. She was feeling better now. She had new plans.

Kayleigh's body oozed arousal she hadn't experienced for a long time. The deserved killing of that thoroughly obnoxious entity was so fulfilling. On top of that, she knew from past experience that it was counterproductive to stifle these ongoing desires. But, at this moment, she needed gratification of a more conventional kind. And what Kayleigh wanted, Kayleigh, by hook or by crook, she always got. Then, she acknowledged, there was the small matter of the Patron Saint of Lost Causes standing in her way. Whatever, Kayleigh thought, attempting to garner confidence.

Chapter 18

Friends

As soon as Cat walked into the ICU, it was apparent things were not normal. The on-duty receptionist beckoned Cat.

'What on earth is going on, Sue?'

'Haven't you heard? You're so not going to believe this. They've found Dawn Jacques guilty of murder!'

'Dawn? Murder? Murder of whom, for God's sake?'

'Her husband!'

'Come off it!'

'It's true. Everybody's talking about it.'

'So that's what all the fuss is about. Blimey. I . . . I just can't believe she'd . . . I dunno . . . that she'd be capable.'

Cat's legendary instinct immediately kicked in. She suddenly thought of Spot's disappearance the previous night.

The more she thought about it, the more a plan formed. I must try to communicate with Spot. The strengthening telepathic bond just might be strong enough, Cat mused. I'll try with Spot tonight, she decided. Immediately, she felt a rush of anticipation, her positivity reaching new heights.

Over time, the hospital staff came to terms, more or less, with the tragic incident involving their loved and admired colleague, Dawn. Naturally, speculation as to the cause of Dawn's breakdown was rife. A large element cited the unrelenting workload regularly heaped onto the staff's shoulders. Some could cope. Others, clearly, could not.

Cat was passing the corner shop on her way home when she suddenly remembered something she needed. Whether the strange shopkeeper would have what she required was not guaranteed, but she thought it was worth a go. There was no queue; it was just before closing time. Kayleigh was tired after a long day, but she still produced that winning smile. She had been waiting for this next visit.

Cat asked, 'Now, this is a long shot—'

'We like a challenge,' Kayleigh interrupted, tantalisingly.

Cat carried on. 'I've broken my nail file. It was only a cardboard thing. You don't happen to sell them, do you?'

The shopkeeper raised a forefinger in a gesture that suggested she might just have something. 'Wait, a sec.'

Kayleigh reappeared armed with a nail file. She placed it on the counter for Cat's approval.

'Crikey!' muttered Cat, 'Metal—that's much better.'

'You could do some damage with that,' Kayleigh chuckled.

On returning home, Cat let the desperate dog out of the back door, whereupon he instantly relieved himself.

'Sorry, Spot! Come on then, off to the canal.' Spot hesitated.

'Come on, Spot! What's up?'

He looked up at his owner and attempted to convey his recent frightening experience.

Cat was on it. 'Okay, Spot, tell me about it. You saw someone, didn't you, on the canal?'

He dipped his head, as if in confirmation, and led her to the bowl and doggie goodies, which she'd bought from the shop. She understood it now: a lightbulb moment.

'It was Kayleigh, wasn't it?'

The little Jack Russell rubbed his nuzzle against her hand.

Cat's instincts kicked in. *Yes! Good old Spot. Could this*

be connected to the murders and Declan's innocence?

Unusually, Roxette was ahead of time on her way to her fabulous workplace. Passing the corner shop, she paused, thinking, I need a bottle of wine for tonight. Shiraz, I think, for a change.

She made a ninety-degree turn and entered the emporium. Expecting to see Kayleigh, a stranger appeared. It was almost closing time.

'Hi, I'm Connie, Kayleigh's assistant. How may I help you?'

As Roxy tendered her order, the grey, shimmering Being that was Kayleigh floated out from the storeroom, barely touching the floor.

'I'll take over now,' the Being ordered. 'Your wine, my lovely.'

Her easy reply entranced Roxy. 'Why, thank you, Kerry, isn't it?'

'Kayleigh.'

Roxy felt her legs giving way. She'd never experienced feelings like this before. She was falling, inwardly crying, *Help, someone!*

Kayleigh, while appearing calm, was beside herself. She saw a future with this gorgeous example of the human race, and she couldn't wait to get on with it.

'What's your name?' Kayleigh asked the nymphet. 'You don't need to know my name. Come on!'

Kayleigh, taking Roxette to another place, glanced at her assistant. Connie instantly understood—she knew which side her bread was buttered. She shut the shop up, checked all was well, and picked her way home.

Roxy, silently apologising to Cat, was in heaven—or was it hell?

Connie had cunningly slipped her legs under the table, gaining the respect and trust of her superior. Perhaps now was the time to capitalise on her efforts. Many throwbacks and new homers populated this small village. Connie smiled to herself. Might this be the time to instigate her own murky agenda? That jumped-up cocky plumber needed bringing down a peg or two. But it hadn't escaped her notice that her boss had developed similar intentions.

'Take a seat,' Kayleigh offered, gesturing towards a comfortable sofa. Roxy needed no encouragement, immediately flopping into the welcoming cushions with grateful abandon.

'I bet you're a red girl.'

'I'll drink whatever I can get!' was Roxy's default reply.

Kayleigh placed herself next to the radiant creature. Intoxicated by the wine and the situation, Roxy gave herself up.

The ensuing embrace totally consumed them. Nothing else mattered now. The physicality of the moment transcended everything they had experienced before.

Lying back, it became clear it was a time for reflection. It had been a long time since she had felt those earthy feelings.

Roxy was less sure, 'Wow! That was incredible,' she breathed. But a sudden feeling of guilt rose within her. She shouldn't. Cat might be sympathetic—or would she?

Roxy was a simple soul with natural instincts. But she had no choice. She would have to tell her new lover it couldn't continue.

'Okay, my beauty, sometimes, things are not to be,' retorted Kayleigh, faking a sigh. *Déjà vu,* she thought; her mind returning to that fabled era when things were so much simpler. Kill or be killed.

And with that, the naïve young woman departed, thinking only of the love of her life—Cat.

Incandescent didn't even come close. As the door clicked shut, Kayleigh flew into a way-off-the-planet fury. Woe betide anyone who might cross her path now. The familiar resurgence of love versus hate reared its head again. She loathed Roxette for deserting her, yet relished the chance of exacting her revenge.

'My latest disappointment must pay the price,' she determined.

On her way home the next evening, Roxette called in to see Kayleigh. She needed to apologise for her charade. Feeling inadequate, she hadn't a clue where to begin.

Kayleigh was quick on the uptake. With her scheming skills to the fore and her out-of-hand rage, at least for now, under control, she took over the proceedings.

'Roxette! Let's try to work out where it all went wrong. How do you fancy a walk on the canal?'

'When are you thinking?'

'Tomorrow night?'

'Okay, I'll text you when I've finished my shift.'

As dusk descended, an unnatural pang in Spot's gut roused him from slumber. His senses recognised bad news. Springing out of his basket, he headed over to Cat. She was dozing, tired again from a particularly arduous day. He nuzzled her hand and recalled the scent of the man.

She woke with a moan. Disoriented, she glanced at her watch. It was 15.30.

'Hey, Spot. Goodness, I must have dozed off.'

Spot's look was intense. *It's more serious than that. Someone is in trouble. We need to help, quickly.*

Sensing Spot's distress, Cat rushed to put her coat on. They were out of the door in a flash, running to the canal, fearing someone's life might be in danger.

Kayleigh grabbed Roxy's beautiful neck, anticipating her glorious revenge. An approaching dog barked repeatedly, distracting her. Spot, closely followed by a breathless Cat, arrived at the scene in the nick of time. Spot snarled, bared his teeth, and went for his enemy's leg, clamping his jaws around it.

Kayleigh shrieked.

Seeing her allies rushing toward her, Roxy felt empowered. She elbowed her assailant in the ribs, seized the arm wielding the weapon, and smashed it against a tree. The knife flew out of Kayleigh's grasp, describing a perfect arc before falling into the canal.

Just as Kayleigh prepared to retaliate Cat felt the nail file in her pocket. She grabbed it and thrust it into Kayleigh's body where she knew it would do maximum damage—her kidneys. The murderess slumped to the floor, leaving Roxy free to live another day.

'Come on! Let's get out of here,' Cat panted, adrenalin pumping. Roxy, still shaking from her narrow escape, followed on.

Arriving home, Cat wondered whether to call the police, but dismissed the idea instantly. They probably wouldn't believe her version of events, thinking she was the villain.

Cat welcomed her shaking but defiant lover inside. Roxy collapsed onto the settee, proud of her new-found positivity, and recalling the turn of events that had occurred since the last time she was here.

Cat's respect for her lover soared to a new level now.

'Roxy, I'm so proud of you. That took guts.'

'You inspired me Cat. That's always been the way.'

With that, Roxy's pent-up shock at her narrow escape overwhelmed her. Cat came to the rescue, her love for this creature interminable.

The fading light cloaked Kayleigh's unsteady gait. No one she passed noticed her, or if they did, probably thought she was drunk.

She crashed in, and grabbing a towel, pressed it hard against her wound in a desperate attempt to stem the flow of blood. That done, she downed a few powerful painkillers and confined herself to bed, thanking her lucky stars for making it back to a safe place of recuperation, and hoping she would live.

The fury of the attack shocked Kayleigh to the core, but given the circumstances, contacting the emergency services was out of the question. She told herself to get a grip. Quite how her erstwhile customer and that wretched dog had got wind of her dastardly plan, she had no idea. She had harboured deep reservations about the nurse's capabilities, but nothing prepared her for the reality. And the bimbo: *What the hell is going on? I wasn't expecting that!*

Before she shut her eyes, an unwelcome thought told her she'd need more than just rest to get out of this predicament.

Chapter 19

Janice

In the days that followed, Kayleigh press-ganged Connie into holding the fort, but things in the shop went steadily downhill. The assistant wasn't a people-person, totally apathetic to the flotsam and jetsam drifting in and then out again. Although she was vaguely interested to know how her soon-to-be ex-boss had come by her injury, honestly, she didn't really give a damn.

An elderly lady entered the shop, eager to purchase her pooch's favourite food. Looking around, she asked the new assistant at the counter, 'No Kayleigh today?' Connie, phone in her face, reluctantly addressed this irritating interruption.

'Oh, she's not feeling herself at the moment,' was the minimum rejoinder.

'Oh, I'm sorry to hear that,' the loyal customer said. 'I hope she'll be back on her feet soon. Please give her my best. Have you any Doggy Delight?'

Connie, still engrossed in her phone, never even acknowledged this request. Instead, letting out a heavy sigh.

The lady got the message and, disappointed, departed empty-handed, muttering, 'Looks like it's 'Abduls' then.'

The footfall eased off.

'How's the shop going? Are you coping?' asked a weary, pasty-looking Kayleigh, staggering in from the back room.

Connie, with other things on her mind, merely shrugged her shoulders. 'Oh, you're up! Yeah, fine,' she replied indifferently.

By the end of the week, the Being inside Kayleigh had to ask for help. She had no choice. Connie remained silent about her secret intentions. Watching the boss's strength rapidly ebbing away, she sensed her chance was approaching.

The blue lights arrived. Connie led the two paramedics upstairs. Taken aback by the state of the patient and inspecting the wound, one of them asked the obvious question: 'How on earth did that happen?'

The paramedics looked across at the loitering female. Connie merely shrugged.

Kayleigh had to think quickly. 'Oh, I had an accident in the kitchen—fell on a knife.'

The long-in-the-tooth medics flashed each other knowing looks.

'Yeah, right!' one said.

'Come on, Ray! Let's get her off to A&E. They can sort her out.'

Jeff hadn't got a lot of time for bare-faced liars. If nothing else, it was disrespectful to those committed to helping them.

As they stretchered her out and slid her into the ambulance, Connie had a thought, *That's got shot of her! She's on a one-way journey, so I reckon I can finally make plans for my forthcoming venture. Goodbye, tedious proletariat and welcome to Madam Condoleezza's house of pleasure where, if you have the money, nothing will be a problem. Unless, of course, you want it to be!*

Kayleigh was in uncharted waters—at the mercy of the medics and her subconscious mind.

A young black nurse came to monitor the new arrival. Despite her condition, Kayleigh couldn't fail to note the nurse's potential.

The nurse looked intently into her patient's eyes, then at the monitors. 'I'll be back shortly, Kayleigh,' she said, fearing the worst.

The Being knew the body she had inhabited for an uneasy, yet enduring tenure was failing fast. Looking around and seeing no one, it became desperate to find a host to continue its unerring destiny.

Kayleigh made her decision. 'When my nurse comes back, I will do whatever is necessary.'

The monitors' beeps picked up, heralding the demise of the earthly body. Kayleigh prepared herself. 'This is it!'

The unsuspecting nurse returned and sat down, facing the heavily infected patient. Knowing it only had one option, the Being started the intricate process, summoning every ounce of its strength. The transition was complete. Kayleigh's Being had morphed into the body of its only hope, Janice. The atavistic Being, for countless ages in attendance of this mortal coil, merely waited patiently to witness the next incantation of this soap opera that was the world.

'Janice: I like that name,' the Being uttered.

Janice suddenly awoke to the noise of the monitors.

'What? I must have dropped off. That's not like me.' She focussed. 'Oh, my God! My patient.'

The machines told Janice it was all over. She felt responsible for not being more attentive. *I could be in a lot of shit here,* she told herself. *I don't know what came over me. What's happening? I've got to pull myself together. The rest of the guys will be in shortly. I need to act normally.*

Sure enough, the door opened, and Dr Ahmed entered. 'We've lost her then, Nurse Janice,' he said, examining the patient and checking her notes. 'From what I can see, it wasn't a surprise, given the advanced infection.'

A relieved Janice breathed a huge sigh of relief and agreed, 'Yes, Dr Ahmed.' He smiled a sympathetic smile.

Janice pointedly checked her watch. 'I'm sorry, doctor. It's past my break time. Could I go now?'

'Okay, write your report first, Nurse Janice, then go for your break.'

Janice recovered her mobile phone from the nursing station and slumped down at her favourite table, her body still shaking.

'Jeez, what the hell went on there?'

As she sipped her coffee, she felt her phone buzz. 'What the hell do you want now? This had better be good?' She was spitting blood. Her partner, on the phone, half apologised for his latest misdemeanours, but it wasn't good enough.

The pathetic response didn't bear a reply. A girl had to do what a girl had to do. Suddenly, she heard Kayleigh's voice in her head: *Janice, you now have powers passed onto you by a former Being. I am the rejuvenated Being who will guide you and help you to right many wrongs.*

'What, little me?' Janice voiced, in la-la land.

Yes, you. But do not be unduly perturbed.

Janice recovered, sort of. If this mind-communication was meant to reassure her, it only left the human with a feeling of *je ne sais quoi.*

In the weeks leading up to this pivotal moment, Nurse Janice had been considering her options both personally and professionally. Her boyfriend was continuing his pain in the arse behaviour and she felt she deserved better; she wanted out. The job had lost its newbie lustre. The system had slowly but surely ground her down to where she felt the urgent need to seek another job.

She began searching on the internet. A position as a nurse in a private medical practice caught her eye. As she scanned the details, with a refreshing emphasis on the patient. This was just what she was looking for—a new start away from the constraints of the dear old NHS. And the money was almost alike. Janice noted the location: Whitby. *Where the heck is that? I've never heard of it. Maybe it's near St Ives.* Janice dreamed optimistically, *I might become a famous artist, they say the natural light there is fantastic!*

She googled the postcode. Alas, it wasn't Cornwall.

'Bloody Hell, North Yorkshire. That's the end of the world, isn't it?' the born and bred Brummie exclaimed.

Although long considered an acquired taste, Birmingham, the UK's second city was enjoying a newfound renaissance and was almost considered fashionable—a prospect unthinkable only a few years ago.

But the more she weighed up the pros and cons, the better the prospects at this possible new location became. The wild, unspoiled seaside, the moors, the much friendlier people, the fish and chips! Janice decided—she would get in touch with the practice the next day. She had a good feeling about this.

The arrangements were complete. Her boyfriend had been relieved of his duties in no uncertain terms, and Whitby was waiting. Janice had handed in her notice and worked the required time. Tomorrow would be the first day of the rest of her life.

The Being was intrigued.

Chapter 20

The Blue Bank Inn

Janice pulled up the covers of her comfortable bed, still buzzing from her first manic evening behind the bar.

As they started tidying up, waiting for the last of the punters to depart, the kindly Mike noted their new barmaid was shattered.

'Hey Janice, you have done brilliantly on your first shift; well done!' Mike said.

Janice demurely replied, 'I hope I'm up to the job, Mike?'

'Oh, absolutely you are. Look, why don't you get off to bed? Ronnie and I will sort this little lot.'

The relieved new barmaid extolled her thanks to Mike and headed for a well-earned kip upstairs. She dropped off to sleep to the sounds of the last of the vehicles exiting the car park, the punters noisily shouting out their goodbyes and slamming doors shut. The constant din of the thriving establishment was finally replaced with a welcome tranquillity. Janice reflected on her life-changing decision to upsticks. The new job as assistant to the amenable Doctor Egton was like the proverbial breath of fresh air. Nothing seemed a problem; if anything, the slower pace of life was mildly frustrating for a girl more used to coping with the constant frenetic schedule of a hospital. Her initial six-month contract was for three days a week only, with the prospect of an extension—depending.

She soon became a tad bored—there were only so many walks along the beach to do, after all. The tiny flat she rented in the town was okay, but she sensed something better was in the air.

Her colleague, Lyn, with whom she'd struck up a friendship, suggested a trip out one night for a drink and a bite to eat.

'There's a cosy little pub in Sleights only about ten minutes' drive away. How d'you fancy it, Jan?'

'Let's go for it!'

They pulled up at the Blue Bank Inn, named after that notoriously steep part of the main road entering the village, on the way to Whitby.

Inside, the convivial atmosphere was particularly welcoming, and together with the roaring log fire, the new friends felt pleased with their choice of venue.

'What's your poison then, Jan?'

'A port and lemon, please.' Janice was pushing the boat out, and why not?

Lyn waited in the queue. And waited and waited. Finally being served, and accepting the genuine apologies from the already overstretched bar person, Lyn ordered two of the same but had to ask the question.

'You don't have any help tonight? By 10.30, you will be good for nothing!'

'Tell me about it. If you know of anyone who fancies a job here, please let me know. There are even two rooms that go with the job, but we still can't get the staff!

Lyn set the drinks down on the table nearest the fire. 'Here's to your new job and our continuing friendship!'

'Thanks for that Lyn,' Janice gushed, whilst also expressing an interest in Lyn's job reference.

'I could do that. Gissa job!' Janice joked, assuming her friend would appreciate her Yosser Hughes, Liverpudlian soap reference.

'Huh?' Lyn didn't get it. 'You fancy a job behind the bar, then?'

'Why not?' Janice replied. 'A—I could do with some extra money. B—I would enjoy the company, and C—the rooms above sound like a welcome alternative to that crap flat I'm in at the moment!'

After an enjoyable evening, without overdoing the booze, the girls got up to go. 'I'm just going to have a word with the barperson about the supposed job. I shouldn't be long: the queue has gone down a bit now.'

'Okay, Jan, I'll start the car and get the heater going. Good luck.'

The bar person replied to Janice's enquiry. 'The gaffer, Mike, will be the one to talk to. Ring tomorrow, about 10.30. I'll tell him to expect your call. Your name is ...?'

'Janice. And thank you so much. My friend and I had a great night in your wonderful pub!'

A tired, but elated bar person smiled back, sensing help and company of whatever kind would be more than welcome.

'Let's hope the gaffer agrees ...'

The next morning, an excited assistant headed for the practice. Janice had worked it so that she'd get the chance to telephone the gaffer of the Blue Bank Inn at the agreed time. Hoping the bar person had informed him, that 10.30 was convenient and also if the gaffer was indeed willing to hire an extra bartender. And, again, if the job was as described to her. She privately conceded that was a lot of ifs!

Janice stole away to a remote area and checked to make sure she had a good enough signal on her phone—not always guaranteed in these parts she had discovered. All good.

A booming voice answered: 'The Blue Bank Inn. Mike speaking. How can I help?'

Taken aback by the more than positive tone, Janice announced herself, almost apologetically, as the would-be applicant for any bar job that might arise in the future.

Far from realising Janice's worst fears, Mike jumped straight in. 'Young lady, I have been informed of your interest as a bar person and if you can come down to see me ASAP, I'm sure we can sort something out to our mutual benefit!'

'Wow!' Janice quickly composed herself. 'Is eight o'clock tonight convenient, Mike?'

'Of course,' came the delighted gaffer's reply. 'See you then!'

Janice immediately looked for her pal, Lyn, to impart her news.

'Ha-ha, go for it, girl! Sorry, I'm busy tonight, otherwise, I would back you up in person, but I'm more than confident you will smash it!'

Jan gave her a friendly hug. 'Thanks, Lyn.'

'Let me know how it goes, Jan.'

Lyn was so pleased for her proactive colleague. She felt privileged to be her friend. Jan reminded her of a famous personality. Eyes like saucers, short hair, perfect skin tone and a body to die for. *Got it: Halle Berry.* Lyn sensed this film star look-alike was totally out of place in the sticks and that one day she would fulfil her infinite potential, whatever that might be.

The new Being took this compliment as it was intended. The former Being, however, was unsure what the destiny of her host might be. But it would certainly be interesting to watch it unfold.

Lyn shivered—a sudden, unwelcome chill passed through her. 'I need a cup of tea before I get back to work,' her positive vibes tempered by this strange and unknown experience.

From her room, Janice heard a car door bang shut down below. The dark-skinned beauty was pleased with how things were shaping up and she looked forward to a fulfilling future. Tomorrow was her last day at the practice. Her thoughts wandered to her gorgeous boss, Dr Egton. If he wandered into the pub one night, Janice mused, she would certainly serve him one, at least.

Mike sat down with his new superstar with a coffee after another crazy night. 'Drink this Jan. You look like you need it!'

'Thanks, Mike.'

'Whether by chance or design, young lady, since you arrived . . . '

Janice froze, wondering if this was a 'Dear John' moment.

Mike smiled at this self-deprecating treasure sitting before him, noting her look of horror. He continued: 'Since you arrived, our takings have gone through the roof, and we need help. Janice, I want you to work here full-time; I'll match your wages at the practice, and you can start straight away. What do you say? Please say yes!'

A stunned and thankful ex-nurse immediately replied, 'Yes, please!'

Janice loved her new job—it hardly felt like a traditional workplace. Once she'd got used to the drink-fuelled leers emanating from the other side of the bar and learning to smile engagingly, nothing seemed a problem. Or did it? Janice was streetwise enough to realise that life was not all sweetness and light. The Being inside her agreed.

It was a quieter midweek evening. Three blokes approached the bar and collected their drinks from Ronnie while Janice watched them select the best seats next to the inviting log fire and thought nothing more.

Two lads entered, kitted out in mountain bike gear. Janice served the good-looking one who announced himself as Roy. He gestured to his now-seated mate, Mark. Janice felt an immediate connection with Roy. She flashed him an intense look. Roy sensed an agenda alert.

As the night wore on and the pub filled up, the two bar people went about their business with now seasoned aptitude. A slightly unsteady man appeared in front of Janice and in a slurred tone asked for 'the same again.'

Ronnie took over, remembering what he had previously asked for.

With an embarrassing hiccup, the already pissed chap returned to his table, miraculously, without spilling a drop.

'Come on, then!' the tallest chap said continuing the debate they had been having since they had first encountered the bar person. 'My money is on Ronni Ancona, the actress.'

'No,' the thin one countered, I reckon it's more a Ronnie O'Sullivan; you know, snooker player? He looks like he's got a helluva shot on him!'

They fell about laughing, congratulating themselves on their razor-sharp wit! The third, quietly spoken chap put in his two pennies worth, declaring: 'No, it's a trans.'

More cackling. More ale.

‘Right, watch and learn!’ the larger of the three chaps said, making his move.

Janice knew something was about to go down. glancing across the room she spotted one of the three blokes staggering to the bar, his sights firmly fixed on her colleague. Instinctively, Janice closed up to Ronnie in time to witness the unfolding fracas, first-hand.

The drunken oaf lifted the hinged bar access, lolled up to Ronnie, and grabbed his crotch.

‘It’s not Ronnie O’Sullivan anyway!’ he triumphantly announced. ‘It’s not Ronni Ancona either. My God, maybe it could be a trans after all!’

Janice’s eyes shot across to Roy. Grabbing the offending oaf, Roy wrenched him over the bar, grabbed his hair, and smashed his head against it with unbelievable force.

The oaf’s face now resembled the rare steak chasseur that Roy had consumed previously, Roy dragged him across to his mates’ table, and in front of them, gave his face another bashing against the stone chimney breast. The offensive piece of shit collapsed to the ground, but Roy wasn’t done yet. Aiming a ferocious kick at one of his legs, Roy heard the shin bone crack.

The stunned onlookers—speechless.

‘Right!’ Roy gulped, struggling to catch his breath. ‘Get him and the rest of you out of here now. And if I see you in here again, trust me, I won’t be so lenient.’

They got the message. Dragging the shattered remains of their mate into the frosty night air, they headed for their pickup and scarpered—Roy’s threat ringing in their ears.

The remaining voyeurs finally caught their breath.

Mike crashed into the room: ‘What the fuck?’ came the ready expletive. ‘Just had this joint tarted up, for fuck’s sake.’

Ronnie, recovering, tried to explain, without success.

Janice assumed responsibility. ‘Nothing we can’t handle, boss.’

They all set about tidying up. But as Janice was washing the blood off the desecrated stone fireplace, she could see the writing on the wall. It was time to move on. Roy glanced across at this enigma—the barmaid. She caught his eye—the connection between them growing and which he was certain had somehow empowered him to do what he had just unbelievably carried out.

He found himself uttering words over which he had no control. ‘Janice, you can’t stay here; it’s too dangerous. I live alone, not far from here. Come back with me, at least for tonight, just to be safe.’

Janice stared intently into his eyes, satisfied that she had seen what she was looking for.

Janice explained to Mike the reasons for her decision to quit and thanked him for his understanding.

'Not a problem Janice. You get off home and if you decide pub life isn't for you, I will understand.' He was in awe of this creature who seemed to have powers he had not encountered before.

Janice grabbed him in a warm embrace. 'Thanks, Mike. I won't forget what you've done for me.'

And Janice and Roy were gone, leaving Mike and Ronnie staring at each other. 'Are you going to be okay, Ronnie?' Mike genuinely valued his resilient member of staff.

'Of course, Mike, you kinda get used to these situations, unfortunately!'

'A case of having to!' Mike replied.

Roy eased the Land Rover into his garage.

'Wow, this is in the middle of nowhere,' Janice remarked.

'That's the way I like it—away from prying eyes.' As she stepped across the threshold into the ambience of the toasty living room, Janice knew she had landed on her feet.

Noticing the positive vibes, Roy invited his new friend to take a seat in front of the fire while he went to the kitchen to fix them a nightcap.

They chatted easily, discussing their respective lives and how things might transpire in the future. Roy finally showed Janice her bedroom, wishing her a peaceful night— after the drama at the Blue Bank. He shut her door and made his way to his beautifully appointed master bedroom. The emotions in his head were positive but tinged with a nagging issue. This woman had inspired his actions that night, and while he welcomed the powers afforded to him, he was seriously apprehensive about what else may reveal itself in the future.

Roy was right to be wary of his new acquaintance. Janice, secure now and finally relaxing, turned her mind to plotting her next move.

The smiling Being thought of her first reaction on seeing her new—temporary or otherwise—home, in the middle of nowhere.

Chapter 21

It's Grim up North

Thanks to the doctors and nurses, Declan felt like a new man—ready to take up his place in the circle of life. He'd learned that the Patron Saint of Lost Causes had taken him under her wing. It was her care that had saved his life. He wouldn't be forgetting that anytime soon.

The door to his room flew open. His heroine rushed to his bed.

'Declan!' Nurse Cat cried, 'The police are coming for you.'

'Huh! Why?' Declan spluttered.

'Apparently, you're well enough to face the consequences for what those bastards think you have done,' Cat spelt out.

'Oh, shit!'

‘Declan, listen. We both knew this might happen. And because I believe you’re innocent, I’m going to help you abscond. There’s no alternative. We both have to leave, pronto!’

‘But where shall we go?’ asked a dubious Declan. ‘I’ve contacted my cousin on the North Yorkshire Moors, and he’s unreservedly agreed to take not only me but also a wanted, convicted killer!’

‘You told him that? Crikey Cat,’ Declan acknowledged, ‘I’m looking forward to meeting this guy. He sounds like a proper St Jude. Just like you!’

Cat had also contacted Roxy to meet her in the canteen on her break when she knew it would be quiet. She needed to tell her friend of her plan to set Declan free before the police returned him to unjust incarceration. Cat knew Roxy would be sympathetic to her course of action, but she was fearful of the consequences the devastating news would have on her lover.

Cat told her about their opportunity to stay at a safe bolthole up North and to take their chances out of sight for a while. Cat knew Roxy well enough to trust her with this intel.

‘You have no choice, Cat. Go for it! But . . . I can’t stand to lose you. God knows how long it’ll be before I see you again.’

Roxy sobbed uncontrollably, unable to contain her feelings. Cat immediately cradled her distressed lover—tears welling up in her eyes, too.

'Roxy! Our love will never end, I promise.'

They grabbed each other tight.

Finally, forcing themselves to recover, Roxy said, 'I don't know what to say, except I know we will keep in touch. And I guess we'll just have to see what happens.'

More sobs and more heartache followed as they reflected on their all too brief time together. This would not be the end. No way, Roxy promised, hoping beyond hope, that things would work out fine. Cat determined that, as far as she was concerned, they most definitely would. They held each other's tender gaze and finally parted.

Naresh entered Declan's private room. He caught the patient out of bed, hastily pulling his clothes on, and Cat in attendance.

'What in heaven's name is going on here? I don't remember authorising Mr Mitchell's discharge, Nurse Catherine?'

Show time!

Cat turned to face her hero, not quite knowing where to start.

'Mr Hussain, we both know someone set Declan up as a convenient scapegoat in the murder of the two schoolgirls on the canal. On top of that, he's also a suspect in the double murder of his next-door neighbours. The police are here now. They're on their way to arrest him and return him to prison. He's innocent, I'm sure of it. I can't allow this to happen. I'm going to take him somewhere safe. Please, Mr Hussain! Do you understand?'

Cat and Declan stood anxiously by the door, waiting for Mr Hussain's reaction, and their escape.

'Mr Hussain,' Cat panted, 'I informed you I arranged cover in case something . . . in case this might happen. That time is now. I beg you.'

The kind consultant dropped his head, paused and finally nodded his assent. 'Okay, Cat, Declan, go! I'll phone your cover. Give me the number.'

The out-of-it police guard remained oblivious as they crept past. They were out of there!

Naresh, apprehensive about his future but immensely satisfied that his decision was the correct one, quietly hummed the tune that surreptitiously came into his head: *Que sera, sera.*

'Wouldn't you know it? Somebody's tipped him off!' An irate copper observed, looking at an empty bed.

Turning to his underling, who was supposed to be guarding the killer, a resigned gaffer commanded, 'Get onto HQ, *if* you can do that! He can't have got far.'

Cat was driving. Spot, on the back seat, knew in an instant who this man was.

It was late afternoon. Privately, Declan knew that the range of the electric car was not sufficient to get them to their destination. 'What does it say on the dash, Cat?'

Cat looked down at the battery-level light on her beloved conveyance. It didn't look good.

'Let's pull off the motorway at the next junction. We won't make the services, so we'll just have to take our chances. And Spot looks like he is desperate for a pee.'

At last! Spot thought, fearing a slight accident might be about to happen on the back seat. Cat agreed.

'It's getting dark. I'll have to put the headlights on soon. That will definitely finish the battery off.'

The chances of recharging in this backwater of South Yorkshire looked remote. They exchanged apprehensive looks, thinking they could well be sleeping in situ tonight.

'Hang on, Cat,' Declan burst out. 'I thought I saw a hooked-up VW ID3 back there.'

'Okay, let's take a look,' Cat replied, quite willing to grasp at any straws and trusting him implicitly. She applied the brakes, dramatically executing a tight U-turn with seasoned aplomb. She pulled the car off the road, stopping in front of a set of sturdy-looking metal gates.

Declan eased himself out of the car. 'Here it is, Cat!' he yelled.

And there, set slightly back and to the left of the gates, was a garage, its open doors revealing an electric car on charge. They looked at each other with welcome relief, wondering what stroke of fate had brought them here, in the middle of nowhere!

'My God, how lucky is this!' Cat exclaimed.

Declan felt an irrational sense of foreboding in the back of his mind. 'Yes, it seems like a minor miracle, doesn't it?' he replied. But deep down, he sensed that luck had nothing to do with it. Spot jumped down from the back door and disappeared behind a tree to finally relieve himself.

They marvelled at the substantial farmhouse set a hundred yards down a well-maintained drive. But despite the car charging in the garage, with the curtains semi-drawn, it looked abandoned and dead. Who could tell what secrets might be hidden away? Spot had his own ideas.

Declan pressed a button on the pillar at the side of the imposing gates, assuming it was a bell. Nothing. As this was the only option he pushed the button again. Just as they were resigning themselves to extreme disappointment a click-clunk heralded the slow opening of the electrically operated gates. The mysterious old building beckoned.

Declan felt a compulsion to explore this new destination; *but why?* Spot was keeping his canine antennae on alert.

Apart from this strange stop-off place, Kayleigh came to mind.

'I'll park the Zoe in the garage next to the VW, out of sight of the road,' Cat said. 'I know it's taking a bit of a liberty, but the cops could be on us at any moment.' Cat felt a chill pass through her, 'Come on, Spot, best paw forward.'

They collected their personal items, including Spot's paraphernalia and, with much trepidation, crunched their way towards the imposing property. Only the brightly shining new moon in a cold but crystal clear sky illuminated their way.

After about two or three minutes walk, they arrived at a pillared portico and its large, intricately carved door. Declan yanked the ancient metal bell pull. The intrepid trio waited.

Nothing!

An unseen hooting owl broke the eerie silence. Then another gentle purring sound redirected their attention.

The defiant door groaned open to reveal the striking figure of a man. He smiled, enquiring if they were lost and if he could be of any sort of assistance. Cat, open-mouthed, thought, *Oh my God! I think so.* Clichés abounded. *Tall?*

Yes. Dark? Certainly. Handsome? I think so. He ticked all the boxes. And of course—a stranger!

'Er . . . y-yes, please,' she stammered eventually. 'We're stuck!'

Declan, nonplussed, simply took this new scenario in, thinking only positive thoughts. If this *raison d'être* might provide any sort of gratification for Cat, who was he to stand in her way? For now, at least, he was a free man, and he owed that to a wonderful woman. That was good enough for him.

Cat knew the hunk was appraising her intently. She felt her knees weakening, only too aware of the temptation standing before her. A strong woman that she otherwise was, she tried to pull herself together. Her warm coat and fur-lined collar contributed to an irrational hot flush. She needed to shed her outer clothing, quickly. The man's eyes widened, fixing on her clingy, midnight-blue top, adorned with silver stars. He was transfixed. It was as if no one else existed.

Declan, thinking this may have gone on long enough, contributed a subtle cough. Cat, recovering and smoothing herself down, remembered why they were there.

'Err, excuse me, what's your name?' Cat asked, her breathing gradually returning to normal.

'Cameron,' he replied, luxuriating in this gorgeous young woman's coy embarrassment.

'Hi, Cameron. The battery in our electric car is almost dead. We noticed an electric car charging in your garage. We have a way to go yet. Could we possibly trouble you to let us recharge ours? We'll pay, of course.'

'Oh, I think that can be arranged.' Cameron gestured for them to enter. 'Please, come on in!'

The sparkling lights of the chandeliers only served to enhance the features of this Adonis. Cat had the uncomfortable feeling that forces were working here over which she might not have total control.

'We can get you back on the road first thing tomorrow: not a problem. Meantime, I can offer you somewhere to stay for tonight—and your dog, of course. We've plenty of room.'

Cameron offered his hand for Spot to sniff. The gesture met with approval.

'You're all looking tired and hungry and your options in this neck of the woods are limited, to say the least.' he said jauntily, trying to break the ice.

The pair, laughing, accepted this gracious offer.

'Not any sort of problem,' Cameron assured them. 'Let's go into the kitchen. I'll heat some soup to warm you up.'

After supper, he led them up a stairway, passing through a labyrinth of corridors before ushering them into a beautifully appointed bedroom themed in blue.

‘I’ll leave you to it. If you need anything, just pull that.’ Pointing to a cord by the side of the huge four-poster bed.

The visitors thanked him again, and he left, pulling the heavy oak door shut behind him with a hefty clonk.

‘My, what a guy!’ Cat breathed, more than slightly unnerved by her schoolgirl reaction to a total stranger.

Declan looked around the Regency period room. The grandeur of the furnishings, the inviting bed, adorned in matching blue. The silk sheets folded back in a welcoming fashion. Very impressive, yet he simply couldn’t shake off his misgivings about the place.

‘This room wasn’t prepared by accident,’ observed Cat, noting the attention to detail that someone had afforded. ‘This is the work of a fair-handed being.’ Declan, showing a look of puzzlement and then strange realisation, nodded in agreement.

The decision to enjoy this impromptu moment was inevitable. What the hell! This sort of thing doesn’t happen every night!

Spot agreed. Eying up a comfortable chaise longue, he jumped onto it, imagining himself as King Spot the XIV. Making himself at home, Spot thought to himself, *Mmm, I could get used to this.*

Cat and Declan felt a deep love for each other, entirely comfortable in each other's company. They had decided, from the moment Declan began to recover, that their relationship would remain strictly platonic. There was simply no need for anything more. It would complicate things unnecessarily and ultimately have the potential to ruin the special bond that existed between them.

They undressed, and without a hint of embarrassment, slid in between the luxurious sheets. Cat was elated. Declan less so, knowing that somehow, he would need all of his returning strength in the future—physically and mentally.

The visitors were drifting off to sleep when a remote cry of anguish reached them. Perplexed and hearing nothing more, they dismissed it as imaginary, or probably a fox. They'd had an intense day after all, and their brains were scrambled.

A fox? Nope. Imaginary? Spot wasn't so sure.

Chapter 22

The West Wing

Cameron's wife long ago banished to the West Wing, sensed her opportunity to confront Declan, her potential saviour.

The love of her life used to adore her, setting her on a pedestal to admire forever.

'Those were the days; when my meticulously engineered plan to entrap my future husband seemed to work,' the beauty murmured, unexpectedly desperate for a sympathetic shoulder to cry on. 'Then it all went horribly wrong.'

The conniving wretch stopped to reconsider. The entity with similar powers to her own had entered her domain. She had summoned him and his companion, after all. She'd sensed that Declan and Kayleigh were intertwined. And now he was under her roof. Her husband might not approve, but opportunities like this were few and far between.

Cat and Declan were drifting off to sleep when another sound, this time metallic, woke them. The bedroom door opened slowly. Caught in the shimmering moonbeams, a silvery spectre floated into the room. She hovered in front of them with a forlorn look of longed-for anticipation.

'Declan, Kayleigh! Help me, please!'

In an instant, the pleading apparition morphed into human form, adorned in an eye-catching, silver-grey gown, and Cameron appeared behind her. He placed his hand on his wife's shoulder and coaxed her away, voicing an apology to the astounded couple, who simply rubbed their eyes in disbelief.

Her strange, beautifully crafted porcelain face held a look of total confusion as a desperate voice from the past cried, 'Don't leave me!'

'Come on, dear! Let's get you back to bed,' her keeper said, gently shepherding his disorientated wife back to the West Wing and her life of eternal remorse.

Cat and Declan exchanged dumbfounded looks. Spot, on his throne, declined to comment, leaving it to his 'subjects' to deal with. He had enough on his mind. Declan whispered to his dazed pal, attempting to lighten up the situation, 'I think we might have stumbled into the land of the fairies!'

Cat shook her head, 'God knows,' she replied, half smiling, half numb with shock at what they had just witnessed.

Aware of the challenges ahead, she said, 'Let's grab a brandy from the cabinet and get some sleep, like the car we need to recharge.' And then she thought of that dreamy stranger, again.

'Good idea,' Declan agreed.

But just as she dozed off, Cat remembered those ghostly words: *Declan, Kayleigh! Help me, please!*

'We'll sort it tomorrow,' Cat decided. That's all her cluttered mind could think of before drifting off to the land of the fairies. King Spot the XIV simply observed, enjoying his, albeit temporary, reign.

The sun came up, its warm rays streaming in through the window, heralding a new day for the fugitives.

'Oh my God, where are we?' a disoriented Declan demanded to know.

Cat and His Majesty joined in the confusion as they looked around at the luxurious but alien surroundings. Then reality dawned. They lay there wondering what the hell would happen next.

'One egg, or two?' Cameron asked the bemused strangers after knocking on their door and opening it anyway, with no acknowledgement from inside. Incredulous, but thankfully, not in a compromising situation, they thanked the enigma profusely but politely declined, explaining their need for speed.

Cameron smiled his understanding and bowed out.

Debating the motivation behind Cameron's unexpected and uninvited entrance to their bedroom, Declan made a quick decision.

'Time for a sharp exit.'

Cat was on it. Spot followed, feeling slight disappointment that his temporary time as revered aristocracy might finally be over. They were making their way downstairs when they bumped into their host. They thanked him for his hospitality and apologised again for their hasty departure.

'Cameron, how much do we owe you for your kind hospitality—not least, the use of the car charger?' Declan asked as Cameron walked them to the door.

'Oh, don't worry about it. It's been good to see some new faces. I hope you feel rested. Good luck for the future.' They shook hands warmly.

'Hey!' Cameron called after them. 'If ever you are in the area again, please feel free to call in.'

Cat and Declan both acknowledged this seemingly genuine gesture, but …

'What in God's name went on there?' Declan quizzed Cat, as he raced them away in their reactivated car. He wanted to know if Cat had picked up a hint of his hidden powers. He would tell Cat, but now was not the time.

'No idea,' Cat answered simply. 'It's strange, but it seemed they were expecting us. And the apparition?' Cat continued, 'Did I imagine that?'

Declan shrugged his shoulders; of course, he had seen it, too. Changing the subject, he added, 'Well, at least we got the car charged and a good chance of making it to our destination.'

Cat turned to Spot. 'Good boy, Spot.' Spot whimpered.

'What is it, boy?'

Be careful! he conveyed.

Chapter 23

Hope?

Gromont and Cat's kind cousin were reassuringly within reach. Cat allowed herself to relax a little, feeling that things could be hopeful for her wonderful, mysterious companion at last. But then there was the small matter of Declan's enigmatic past. She decided that when an appropriate moment came up, she would invite him to tell her his recollections if indeed he would be ready to do that. *Who knows what's going on in that traumatised mind?* she wondered. *And the small matter of the ghost appearing to know Declan and Kayleigh. Why did she call me Kayleigh? How the hell does she fit into this, anyway?* No matter, Cat would continue to love Declan in her own special way. That commitment would never stop, regardless.

They continued their journey, the silent electric car conveying its occupants to a new life—if the cops didn't catch up with them first.

Cat, taking over the driving, looked down at the instruments, estimating that they should have plenty of charge to get to their destination. Declan agreed.

A period of stability was opening up for them. So Declan felt that now might be the moment to broach the subject of his newly discovered, inexplicable powers, with the astute, resourceful woman sitting next to him. *Where to start?* Declan asked himself. *At the beginning, of course.*

'Cat?'

'Yes.'

'I have something to discuss with you about myself that might surprise you,' Declan began gingerly.

Cat thought, *Crikey! I didn't see this coming. What is he going to tell me?*

Declan continued, 'From the time I regained consciousness in ICU and my body started functioning again, actions that were not previously possible manifested themselves.'

'Go on,' an intrigued Cat invited.

'Well, put simply, somehow, I gained a telepathic instinct. I realised I could read the future and connect to persons or beings of similar persuasion.' Declan's voice trailed off.

Recovering from this revelation, Cat ventured, 'Oh, my sweet. What you are saying is, the scenario we've just encountered didn't happen by chance?'

Declan paused, and rethinking, replied, 'No, I don't believe it did.'

'But who is Kayleigh? Where does Kayleigh come into it, Declan?' asked Cat, nonplussed.

'Trust me, Cat. One thing at a time, Love. That can wait for now. We've got enough on our plate at the moment; you and me.'

Cat immediately bought into Declan's situation. She and her furry companion, Spot, knew a thing or two about telepathy. It was real, and now it was here, a valuable tool in their quest to free a wronged human being.

An excited Cat saw a future where victory for a maligned Declan might be within their grasp. Spot, nestling on the back seat, sighed his approval. Cat sensed that with the trio's combined resources, they might just have a fighting chance ensuring justice would finally prevail and Declan would become a free man. Spot was certain. Nevertheless, caution pervaded. It was important not to get ahead of themselves. The task at hand was to make it to their next port of call before any pursuers had other ideas.

Twenty-five miles to go.

They approached a small settlement. The satnav seemed a tad confused.

'Technology, eh?' Declan sighed. Cat took a turn that seemed logical but ended up in the middle of a busy town. Not what they wanted. It was that time in the morning when parents were hurrying their kids to school, not daring to be late.

As they approached the school crossing, a couple of kids were engaged in a spat over a ball. It rolled onto the crossing. The portly kid hesitated and attempted to retrieve it. Cat, fearing the worst, succeeded in avoiding him and swerving, carried on.

After a few seconds, she looked in her rear-view mirror. The traffic had stopped at the crossing. She could just make out a flurry of people milling around, but turning a corner, the scene disappeared out of sight. Cat thought nothing of it. They carried on. Declan saw a sign. *York 8 miles.*

'Cat! Stop in that lay by, just ahead! I think we're going totally in the wrong direction.'

Cat pulled up while Declan reset the satnav. Again the refrain, 'Technology, eh?'

'Have you got it now, Einstein?' Cat teased.

'Yeah, cheeky!'

At that moment, they heard a police car siren. They looked over their shoulders. There it was, blue lights flashing, then screeching to a halt immediately in front of them, barring any escape. Two cops sprang out of the 'jam jar' and approached the front doors of their escape vehicle with undisguised steely determination. Cat and Declan, eyeing each other with gutted resignation, assumed this was the end of the road for them and Spot.

Cat and Declan opened their windows, hearts beating hard.

The broad-chested cop asked, 'Would you both exit the vehicle, please?'

Declan didn't understand. How had it come to this? They were miles from home, so why should we get pulled over here?

Cat and Declan looked at each other, gobsmacked. They got out.

The other cop stood next to them while the broad-chested Rambo circled the car as if looking for something.

He came back, remarking to his pal, 'I can't see any damage. This isn't the same car.'

'The same car as what?' Declan retorted.

The cops' tone improved markedly, Rambo explaining to the innocent couple what had transpired. 'There's just been an RTA back in town. A car collided with a school kid who was larking around on a pedestrian crossing. He wasn't badly hurt, but the car must have sustained minor frontal damage. More importantly, it didn't stop.'

'I'm so sorry to hear that,' Cat said. 'Is the kid going to be alright?'

The cop, noting her genuine concern, thanked Cat for asking. 'You see, Madam, there aren't many electric cars hereabouts.' He continued. 'And witnesses of the accident reported that the offending car didn't make any noise. One suggested it could have been a Renault, like yours. Others said it was a light-coloured VW ID3. Witnesses reported they saw a male driver and a female passenger in each car. Anyhow, we must get on. We need to track the VW ID3 down as soon as possible. Thank you for your time.'

And with that, they left.

Cat and Declan were euphoric at this unexpected conclusion to the fright of their lives.

'We've been let out of jail, free!' Declan gasped. A bark from the rear of the car agreed.

'Declan . . . ?'

Declan frowned, thinking maybe he had missed something.

'Yes, my love. What is it?'

‘The cop said the car that didn’t stop at the accident might have been a light-coloured VW ID3, or whatever you call it. What was Cameron’s car?’

‘A light-coloured VW ID3.’ Silence

I never did like him anyway, Spot thought.

‘My God! A man and a woman,’ Cat said, thinking back to the apparition and her husband, the hunk.

‘They could be stalking us,’ Cat ventured, not sure if this was out of fear or anticipation. Declan’s face said it all.

Cat and Declan kept their eyes open for a pursuing VW ID3 but saw nothing. The police, apart from the false emergency, were, so far, notable by their absence. Perhaps a combination of failed bureaucracy and shrinking budgets contributed to the pursuers’ ineptitude.

Chapter 24

Cousin Roy

The hills of the fabled North Yorkshire Moors presented unexpected challenges for the soft southerners. The incessant rain added to the already saturated ground. On top of that, the less than one-hundred-percent reliable satnav telling them this and that, and giving out its arbitrary advice, was an added drain on the battery. The heater didn't help. Then the overworked windscreen wipers inevitably triggered the warning light. And if that wasn't enough, another obstacle loomed.

'My God! That looks deep,' Cat said, staring at the swollen stream.

'Come on, Cat, keep it going!'

'Okay, okay, I'm doing it, for God's sake!' Cat cried, as she gamely resisted the fast-moving torrent pulling the car sideways and into impending disaster.

'Through!' Declan punched the air.

The warning light upgraded to critical.

'Come on, car! It can't be far now,' Cat implored.

Turning a corner, they saw an old, crumbly stone house accompanied by the source of the problem they had just successfully negotiated—a babbling brook.

'Wow!' Cat exclaimed, remembering her premonition of this very scene. *You have reached your destination,* the errant computer announced, as though asking for redemption.

Cat pulled the car into the cavernous garage. The trio felt an unprecedented surge of relief. As she pulled out her fob and locked the car, a pool of oil defacing the floor of the otherwise immaculate environment caught the sight of the driver's eye.

Cousin Roy, alerted by the activated security light, observed the scene from the lounge window. His life, so far, unfulfilled, but with his cherished, unrequited secret love finally at hand, he felt things might just be changing. And that boded well. Or did it? A former kissing cousin relished the upcoming events, whether good, bad, or indifferent. Naturally, Cat had an inkling of her cousin's secret desires. Cat flew out of the car into Roy's welcoming arms.

Declan freed Spot, who immediately found somewhere discreet to relieve himself.

'And this is Declan Mitchell,' Cat said, introducing her friend. 'Watch out though, he's a cold-blooded murderer. Can't you tell?'

'Ha-ha! Welcome, Declan! If cuz Cat has you in tow, then I'm not worried.'

Roy led them inside. Again, Declan couldn't believe their luck to receive such a warm welcome in their desperate circumstances.

'Come on in and make yourselves at home. I've gained a new friend,' Roy announced to his, he thought, soon-to-be impressed visitors.

Cat was more than intrigued. 'Where is she?'

'*She's* popped out to get some groceries, but should be back shortly,' he replied, smiling. 'I'll text her to tell her we have visitors—we'll need more stuff for supper.'

The chill in the air required Roy's attention. He always relished this log-burner moment.

'Let me do it,' Cat insisted, her life in a big city denying her any sort of opportunity to connect with a more basic way of living.

'Okay, cuz, go for it!'

Roy supplied her with the necessary sticks and logs to start the fire and in no time, a warm glow illuminated the room. The magical log burner, with its unrelenting energy, seemed to encompass the goal of the newly established allies. The small dog noted a thick, royal blue mat positioned directly in front of this amazing fire-breathing contraption. That's for me, the Jack Russell, aka King Spot XIV decided, curling up on it in heavenly bliss.

'Comfy, are we, Spot?' Cat teased.

Spot replied, in the way he knew Cat would read him, *Yes, this is the life!*

'So, Roy,' Cat enquired, 'how are you since your folks passed away?'

'Oh, thanks for asking. You probably heard they were both extremely ill. They went downhill so fast that it got to the point where, sorry to say, it was a blessing. Oh, well . . . life must go on, I guess. So,' he continued, sucking in a breath, and changing the subject, 'I used to be more than occupied with my business: plumbing, heating, bathrooms, kitchens, pretty much anything really.'

Cat acknowledged his grief but went along with his new tack. 'Well, yes. Judging by the wonderful refurb of your house, your skills seem pretty extensive—and top quality.

'Thanks! I'm cracking on a bit in years now, so I've scaled my business right back. I'm not actively looking for work anymore. Just doing small stuff and emergencies.'

'That's a pleasant position to be in,' Cat noted. 'And you don't look too bad on it!'

'Thanks, Cat. And it helps that my dad left me a sizable inheritance, which more than keeps me in curry and wine!'

'Ha-ha. Long may it continue!' Cat said.

Cat and Roy were reminiscing; sharing childhood memories of a simpler time in their lives when a door opened and a smiling woman announced, 'Hi, everyone! I'm back!'

Roy, proud as punch, gestured towards the radiant, captivating girl standing in the doorway.

'Let me introduce Janice,' Roy said enthusiastically. The visitors' eyes widened, wowed by Janice's entrancing appearance.

'Hi, there! Hi, Janice,' they said, getting up to shake her hand. Spot backed away with a guttural snarl.

A moment was all it took for Janice's inner Being to home in Declan. It was not best pleased.

Ignoring Cat, she moved towards Declan, shook his hand and with a thin, piercing, alien voice said, 'Ah, Declan! At last.' Her grip was icy.

The colour drained from his face. 'Kayl-?' he began before crumpling to the floor.

'Oh, my God! Declan,' Cat cried. 'Roy! Water, quickly!' Cat, in nurse mode, leapt to the rescue.

Janice looked on, unmoved. 'Declan, you should be dead!' the Being inside her declared. 'I promised I would make you pay—and I always keep my promises.'

Roy came back with the water. 'What on earth happened there?'

'It must be the strain of the journey,' Cat said. 'He's still on medication. Maybe it's overdue, but I'm sure I kept up with his doses.'

She looked up at Janice. 'Do you know him?'

'Well, I saw the scars on his face and remembered that there was talk in the hospital of an RTA trauma patient who'd had a lot of plastic surgery.'

'So, you're a nurse, too? In the same hospital as me?'

'Used to be—you were in ICU, I think. I was on the general wards. Look, I'd better get supper on the go before we all pass out.' Janice disappeared into the kitchen. Everyone else—gobsmacked.

Cat couldn't resist the opportunity Janice's absence afforded. 'Where did you meet her, Roy?'

'In a pub. She was working at the bar. There was a fracas. I saved the day and seemed to have impressed her. Shush! She's coming back.'

Declan came round, cradled in Cat's arms, mind in a daze. 'Jeez, what happened? I had a flashback of some sort. I thought I saw, I dunno, some kind of ghost. She was in a silvery-grey gown floating by a river or a canal, maybe. And a strange voice ... '

'Hey, Declan! Don't worry,' Cat assured him. 'You're a bit concussed, that's all. Your head will clear soon. All you need is a stiff brandy and some food. Then you'll be as right as rain.'

Cat was disturbed. That name again; *Kayl ...? Yes, Kayleigh,* she was sure of it.

After enjoying the carefully prepared supper, the visitors relaxed into a welcoming ambience. The physically and mentally powerful Being, Janice became increasingly irritated. So, she thought it was about time to make her presence known. She flashed a commanding, it's-time-for-bed-now look at Roy.

Roy, faking a yawn, cut into the congenial conversation, 'Err ... guys, it's getting late. You'll find your room upstairs, Cat. I left the door open ... ' Roy's voice trailed off. He had wanted to catch up with his cousin, but that would have to wait. 'Mi casa es su casa, as they say in Spanish. There's beer and wine in the fridge. Just help yourselves. See you in the morning.'

This newly-created Being embraced the enticing experience of new targets from which to choose, while the Kayleigh inside her devised tailor-made plans for her former lover, Declan.

An unlikely adversary sensed this decision. *Over my dead body,* Spot thought. He'd only briefly encountered Cat's apparent, previously intended, but from what he had witnessed, Roy seemed a salt of the earth sort of guy. He wasn't a problem. However, the Jack Russell would watch, wait and be ready to pre-empt any initiative of this new Being to impose its devilish authority.

Although uneasy at Janice's presence, Spot settled into his comfortable surroundings and considered his game plan. Kayleigh was ultimately found to be vulnerable. But the beguiling form of life now threatening the status quo seemed somehow more capable. *Was Kayleigh lurking in her, too?* Spot had survived so far; learning as he went along.

Chapter 25

Absolute Power

The recently relocated mates availed themselves of the inviting seats in the backyard of the police house. There was a chill in the air, but the lack of wind and the stunning sunset warmed their hearts. The view over the valley took in the distant farm. Tractors were working the fields. Horses grazed the idyllic pastures, and everything seemed well with the world.

'I think we've landed on our feet here, Greeny,' the senior cop observed.

'You're not wrong, Chalky. The grime of the city seems to be well and truly left behind,' the cockney geezer conceded.

Chalky's mobile splintered their peace. The still-keen, southern pro pulled it out of his pocket, his face quickly returning to police-default-setting. He was a company man, after all.

His expression darkened as he listened intently to the voice on the other end.

'Come on then,' his equally ambitious partner inquired. 'What is it?'

'There's a fugitive on the run.'

'Yeah, so?'

'He's somewhere in Yorkshire.'

'We're in Yorkshire!'

'Yeah, exactly!'

For Chalky, the ambitious wide-boy, an immediate opportunity for promotion beckoned. His aspiring equal, Greeny also relished the prospect, thinking, *There is gold in them there hills, after all.*

They both sensed blood. Although they complemented each other personally and professionally, there was an unspoken rivalry, which occasionally threatened to get out of control.

Cluck, cluck, cluck! Another day, another egg—the alien noise disturbing the townies. Cat half woke. After the last few days, she wasn't sure where she was. She rubbed the sleep from her eyes and yawned. *Of course! The wild moors of the North were now their temporary refuge from the imminent arrival of the hunters.*

Declan, still slumbering next to her, supplied reassurance in the form of a wonderful arm around her body. She had to cuddle him.

Coming around, he murmured, 'What is it, my love—time for my medication, already?' Declan found it difficult to shrug off the confines of his prolonged life in medical incarceration.

Sounds of activity from below reached their ears, prompting not exactly panic but an awareness that they were on the run and their wits had to be constantly engaged. It was only Roy washing up the relics of last night's truncated celebratory dinner.

Panic over—time to freshen up. The en suite bathroom was impressive. Roy, the builder, cut no corners in the careful refurbishment of his pet project. Every task that he'd engaged in, he completed to the highest of standards. The performance of Cat's luxuriant shower confirmed that Roy's obsession was wholeheartedly delivered.

Roy, in charge of breakfast, served up scrambled eggs and brown toast. The grateful visitors consumed his culinary offerings with relish. In contrast, Janice contented herself with a single glass of an acquired taste: pink grapefruit juice. Einstein, aka Declan, fiddled with his iPad, not trusting the established terrestrial propaganda outlet, the TV, to deliver accurate information to the proletariat. A breaking news story leapt to his attention.

> *Police are on the alert to apprehend a killer who recently absconded from a secure hospital in the Midlands. We advise the public not to confront this extremely dangerous individual but to contact their local police department at the earliest opportunity if they have any suspicions, however inauspicious.*

Declan adjusted his iPad. 'Look at this Cat! Taken 'em long enough, hasn't it? Rambo and his uninformed mates had us, and then let us go!' Declan couldn't resist the opportunity to put the boot into his erstwhile torturers.

'I guess we delayed them by turning around because of the satnav error,' Cat noted.

'Well, we need to lie very low now. That's for sure,' Declan responded.

The apparently indifferent Janice was absorbing more than just pink grapefruit.

With time, at least temporarily on their hands, the partners in crime reflected on their predicament. Cat, for her part, decided she needed to get back to basics. Another coffee, another conspiracy theory. She was in therapist mode now. 'Declan, someone set you up for a crime of which you have no memory. Do you still have a total mental block?'

Declan became restless—his recently relaxed demeanour unravelling in front of Cat's eyes. She grabbed him, knowing that she had gone too far and fearful of what she thought he might have recalled.

'I'm sorry, Cat. I can't . . . ' Declan wasn't ready, clearly. Cat cupped his face in her hands, inwardly imploring his recuperation to happen sooner rather than later. He quietened. Cat knew when to back right off.

Jeez, this is not going to be easy! Cat thought, with monumental understatement. Declan, gaining inspiration from his hero, forced himself to stay positive.

A vision flashed into Cat's subconscious. 'The police! They were onto us after all! I have to think of an alternative way forward.'

The steady drizzle turned to sleet, and as dusk fell, snow soon clothed the wild landscape in a blanket of white.

They were sitting together in the lounge when Janice suddenly leapt up, announcing her intentions to the startled friends. 'I need to get some essentials from the shop in Sleights before the weather closes in.'

Roy knew the trusty Land Rover was up to it. 'I'll just check the oil before you go, Jan.'

Pulling up outside the shop, Janice noted that the weather had deteriorated significantly, the road now covered with a thick layer of pristine snow. In the deserted shop, she made her purchases quickly and paid at the till. She was approaching the door when an angry-looking individual barged in; his police uniform covered in snowflakes. She froze, recalling the scene at breakfast and sensing her opportunity.

Greeny, the lustful chauvinist that he was, stopped in his tracks, immediately acknowledging the young woman's remarkable resemblance to movie icon, Halle Berry. He stood in the doorway, deliberately, with the excuse of brushing off the snow from his uniform. Janice took a steadying breath, and as she pushed awkwardly past him, she chanced him a 'come on!' His demeanour softened. Ignoring his better judgement, Greeny's eyes followed her progress as she picked her way gingerly over the snow-covered path.

Wow, what a looker! he thought.

'That wasn't too difficult,' Janice concluded as she threw her shopping into the 4x4.

The police had parked their car behind hers. She didn't panic unduly. *Even the local plod has to eat,* she mused. She climbed in and headed home.

The officer finally came out of the shop and crashed into the jam jar, slamming the door shut.

'Hey! Careful, Greeny!' Chalky spat out. 'By the way, did you notice that girl coming out as you went in?'

'Did I just! What a stunner!' Greeny enthused.

'Typical! Trust you to notice every bit of skirt,' Chalky snapped back.

Greeny pressed on with the business in hand, regardless of the negative vibes directed at him. 'The point is, Chalky, there's a clue here. The missive we received regarding the man on the run mentioned that a dark-skinned nurse also went AWOL at the time of his escape, as did another red-headed nurse, as it happens.'

'So, do you think the looker in the shop could be that nurse?' Chalky queried, displaying his limited cognitive ability.

'Well, without wishing to sound racist,' Greeny remarked, 'how many black girls have we noticed up here?'

'I guess you have a point,' Chalky conceded.

As they pulled away, they noticed a large patch of oil in the pristine snow where the woman had parked her car.

'Follow those oil drips and chunky tyre tracks!' commanded Chalky, still angry but excited at the prospect of bagging a hot suspect.

He sensed something was in the air. Janice, on the other hand, was certain of it.

The ageing, road-going police Ford had no off-road capability, and it soon became clear to Greeny, at least, that caution would need to be exercised here. But then, the world's greatest driver was behind the wheel, and therefore, what could possibly go wrong?

They slithered along, finally spotting the Land Rover—oil leaking out—cautiously pitting its way in the thickening snow.

Encouraged, Paddy Hopkirk, aka Chalky, pressed on, imagining himself on the Monte Carlo Rally with the finishing line just around the next bend.

'Please God, have mercy on us,' Greeny prayed.

Chalky's target came back into view for a brief moment before disappearing over a narrow river bridge.

'I'm going for it,' Paddy said to himself.

The police car shot forward, but there was a sharp bend before the bridge. The car, devoid of any grip in the deep snow, failed to negotiate the bend. Instead, it headed perilously straight on, colliding with the upright of the bridge, rebounding and flipping onto its roof, finally coming to rest upside down in the middle of the swollen, raging torrent.

Janice glanced in her rear-view mirror and sucked in a breath. A damn police car. She had just driven over the bridge when her eagle eyes spotted a gateway. Antennae buzzing, she swerved in and waited for the police car to pass by. Through the mirror, she watched the tragic events unfold. Only the car's wheels were visible. Clearly, there would be no survivors.

Roy opened the door. 'Everything okay, Jan?'

'Everything is going to plan,' Janice asserted, with a malevolent look in the visitors' direction.

Roy, jaw wide open at her obscure reply, somehow sensed that events might run out of his control. His previous misgivings regarding Janice were now being tested. How right he had been to be wary.

Janice made them all hot drinks, and they settled down in front of the log burner, thrashing out the implications of Janice's recent drama. The Jack Russell took it all in.

Cat relaxed, safe, knowing that things would work out. They had to leave this place, but continually running away from the problem would not cure it. An idea came into her head. She would call Roxy the next day and suggest a plan of action. Cat didn't do social media, but Roxy was something of an aficionado in that department. The more she thought about it, the better it got.

Declan could sense Cat's mind whirring away. 'You look positive, Cat. What is it?'

Cat replied, quietly, 'Roxy has the chance to make a significant difference in our quest to vindicate you. And I'm willing to bet she will succeed.'

The perplexed Einstein simply shrugged his shoulders. 'Good . . . I guess.'

'Meanwhile, we have to be gone from here first thing tomorrow. The cops will be pitching up in no time,' Cat asserted.

'Any plans for a destination, Cat?'

'I'm going to call my Auntie Therese in Scotland, now. I'm sure she'll be delighted to see her favourite niece.'

'That's great, but do you think we could get Roy to fix that oil leak first?'

Cat smiled. 'Yeah, of course. The Zoe is no match for Scotland in winter. I hope Roy won't object.'

The blizzard was relentless. The road conditions would delay the discovery of the police car in the river, giving the fugitives time to escape the area in the more-than-capable Land Rover.

Scotland awaits.

Chapter 26

Nowhere to Run, Nowhere to Hide

The fully loaded getaway vehicle pulled out of the drive under an azure sky. Roy knew every inch of the terrain they were about to negotiate. This was just as well, as a foot of snow lay all around, concealing obstacles that could unnerve a less experienced driver.

Janice was alongside Roy, with Cat and Declan in the rear, holding on to the high-level grab handles for dear life. Spot occupied a space in the boot area, securely surrounded on all sides by the baggage.

After an anxious, painfully slow-moving trek, a main road lay ahead. In due course, the A171, with its gritted surface, banished the snow-laden moors to history. The journey to the Queen of the South, with stops, would take them most of the day.

Many of Cat's relatives of Gaelic extraction were dotted around the UK. The fugitives' destination was to be one of them: Auntie Therese lived a few miles out of Dumfries. Right in the sticks and hopefully out of sight of prying eyes.

Roy flicked the radio on. Playing, was a song dear to his heart: Martha Reeves and the Vandellas', 'Nowhere to Run, Nowhere to Hide'. The irony struck a chord with all of them, especially Declan, who now faltered.

The familiar music had triggered in him deeply buried memories of a song with terrible connotations: Belinda Carlyle's, *In Too Deep.* He began shaking again. Cat grabbed him, soothing a look of extreme remorse on Declan's face.

'Oh, my God!' she gasped. 'Are you okay?'

Declan gripped Cat's hands in his. 'Yes,' he finally murmured, sucking in a deep breath. 'I think I'm ready now.'

He knew he had to exorcise the ghostly episode. And he knew Cat would always be there for him. It was now or never.

A soft, reassuring whine came from the boot of the Land Rover.

Declan acknowledged this welcome gesture. 'Thanks, my friend. I'm gonna go for it!'

Roy's eighties-vintage Land Rover was hardly whisper-like, which worked in Cat and Declan's favour. Somehow, they knew they couldn't allow Janice to hear Declan's revelations.

Declan relayed his story from start to finish, Cat variously nodding in assent, questioning the validity, and cringing in incredulity.

'So, Kayleigh killed the schoolgirls, and you got the blame courtesy of DNA on the girl's necklace that found its way into your possession,' Cat concluded.

'Got it, in one!'

The weight Declan felt lifting from his shoulders was massive. He was in a good place at last. But then he shuddered, remembering the unsolved murders of his next-door neighbours. Something was lurking in the deep recesses of his mind. *I couldn't have had anything to do with that, could I? And the electrician? No. Impossible.'*

'I need to talk to Roxy, now.' Cat proclaimed, making Declan jump. She fished out her phone, checked the signal strength and typed a brief message asking her to call back. The response was immediate:

> *I'm on it, Cat. Give me till lunchtime and I will call you. XXX.*

From the moment Cat went AWOL with Declan, a disconnected and distraught Roxy sank into a state of virtual bereavement. The normally bubbly young woman, without a care in the world—until her recent encounter with a would-be assassin—suddenly needed to re-evaluate her priorities. Her social life abruptly halted; she had absolutely no stomach to even attempt to enjoy herself in the absence of her beloved nurse.

'Cat has put her life on the line for somebody else. I have to pull myself out of this dark place and help her, whatever the cost.'

Roxy was comfortable with social media, but she knew this would be out of her league. Racking her brains, she suddenly thought of a former, valued nursing colleague, Emma, who had decided hospital life was not for her.

Roxy picked up the phone. She decided a catch-up drink would provide the perfect opportunity to discuss her bold decision. The door of opportunity was opening. Roxy now felt confident she could relate the stranger-than-fiction episode to the newbie intrepid reporter. Starting from the beginning, Roxy relayed the details, grisly and otherwise, leaving nothing to dispute.

Emma knew, as with any new job, it was advantageous to make a significant first impression. Her gut instincts told her that this out-of-nowhere story might just do the trick.

'Hey! I'm loving this, Roxy. If it comes off; what a feather in all of our caps.' Roxy was thinking the same.

They finished their drinks—and another one. ‘Cheers!’

Chapter 27

Don't Mess With Me

The door opened, and there she was—Aunt Therese, beaming from ear to ear while struggling to restrain her barky Bedlington Terrier.

'*Gad* bless ya, Bab!' she said in her southern Irish brogue. 'Shush, Tara!'

'Oh, Aunt T, it's so lovely to see you. Let me introduce you to Declan, Janice and my Jack Russell, Spot.'

'And Roy! Gad bless ya. Long time, no see. Come inside, all of you. Cummon, Tara, calm down.'

Tara calmed down, instantly feeling comfortable with the new arrivals. A sudden, familiar warmth welled up inside Cat. The enduring fondness revered Aunt Therese had for her niece was Cat's most enduring memory.

'Gad bless ya, Bab!' Aunt Therese repeated. 'Come over here and give me a hug! *Thank you, God, for bringing her here safely!'* she whispered into Cat's shoulder. Yes, there was a God.

'Oh, Aunt T. I can't breathe,' Cat mumbled. Releasing her niece, just a little, she held her gaze,

'Okay, sweetheart, there's nothing much gets passed me. What can I do for you?'

Cat began ...

'Hang on, Cat!' Aunt Therese cut in. 'Let me take Tara into the kitchen, and you can tell me all about it when I've made us all a nice cup of tea. And we'll get something for the dogs. Why don't you come and help me, Gad bless ya!'

Spot, well impressed, took the liberty of nestling in front of the warm fire, anticipating a Scottish treat of some sort. He knew a thing or two about humans—God knows he'd had experience of plenty. *This Irish enigma? Spot on!*

'Your friends seem nice enough, Cat. What does Janice do?' Aunt Therese inquired.

'Oh, she's a nurse.'

'Hmm ... interesting. From the same hospital as you?'

'Yes, but she worked in a different ward. Our paths didn't cross.'

Armed with Rich Highland Shorties, steaming mugs of tea and *McDoggie Delight* for Spot and Tara, Therese and Cat returned to the lounge. There was a sudden lull in the chit-chat. Always quick on the uptake, the historically underestimated Therese felt she must put her intuitive skills to the test. She needed to work out who she was really up against in this newly arrived clan. Aunt Therese raised her eyebrows, casting a *well, out-with-it* look at Cat.

Cat took the hint, took a breath and, breaking the silence, said, 'Aunt T, I have to say, we're all in a bit of a pickle.' Cat explained their circumstances and the inherent dangers.

'Ah, no probs, Cat. Oih could do with a bit of excitement in me *loife*. Now, where is that shotgun that my late husband Jack, God rest his soul, left behind?'

Intrigued by this amazing woman with the heavily pronounced Irish accent, Declan didn't fully take in the implications of these hastily spoken words. Spot, finishing his last morsel, merely felt the vibes—they were only good. Janice, on the other hand, found she couldn't wholly empathise with the assembled company. Therese took note.

Therese had to accept that her hearing was past its best. She'd have to constantly tweak the volume on the telly to hear what was going on. Even Tara had to back away from his nearby seat to insulate himself from the increasing din.

But then, gradually, Therese discovered an alternative. She had learned to lip-read. And in a natural progression, picked up on body language to understand the storyline. In time, this combination bore fruit. Therese, just by analysing Janice's look and demeanour, effortlessly recognised her true colours.

'There'll be trouble here.' Therese acknowledged. 'We just have to be ready for it.'

Cat broke her thoughts. 'Did you say shotgun, Aunt?'

Coming back to the land of the living, whilst applying a knowing look at Janice, Therese responded, 'Oh yes. Jack and I were keen shooters. We were part of a crack team; competing against our local rivals. Jack always appreciated my keen eye and careful touch on the trigger. It rarely let us down!'

Again, another distrustful look was aimed in Janice's direction. Janice, to her credit, met her gaze. And matched the intensity.

'And what were your targets? Clay pigeons?' Cat enquired, gobsmacked, and trying to picture her diminutive aunt engaged in such an unlikely sport.

'Oh, no! The real thing! Pheasants and grouse.'

Cat spotted a mischievous sparkle in Therese's eyes—her Janice conundrum filed away for the future.

Therese loved to prove the cynical, one-hundred-percent wrong, while not contemplating for a minute that her beloved niece fitted into that category. Quite the opposite. Therese realised, straight away, that the newly arrived relative was proving to be a chip off the old block.

'And don't tell me; you owned a black Labrador that faithfully picked up for you, as well?'

'Why yes! Well-guessed, Cat! Gad bless ya, Bab!' the seasoned warrior wisely noted. Cat loved this.

Janice took it all in without comment, understanding this woman had to be respected. She imagined a sort of, *High Noon* scenario where the baddies confront the goodies at the Dumfries version of the *O.K. Corral.*

'Given the choice, I'm with Aunt Therese, thanks!' Janice silently conjectured.

A light-coloured car drew up on the drive. Tara barked as frantically as a Rottweiler. Spot, impressed and in full support, adopted as stern a woof as he could muster. The fugitives, noting the headlights shining into the room, scrambled to peep from behind the curtains. *Had the cops found them already?* The absence of blue lights calmed them.

A man and a woman alighted. Spot immediately recognised the tall, dark, handsome stranger who had effortlessly tempted his heroine back in South Yorkshire.

The dogs were let out, pounding up to the car. Spot, recognising the driver, instructed, 'Back off, Scottie, I think they're okay.'

Tara reluctantly complied, but quizzed, 'Scottie? Huh! Where did that come from?' Then, witnessed by an open-jawed audience, Cameron led his statuesque partner into the house. Aunt Therese took stock of the goddess' radiant beauty, so out of place in their humble Dumfries setting. *This couple looks more like Anthony and Cleopatra than anyone else,* Therese hazarded. The rest of the mere mortals, stunned into silence, also considered they could have just stepped off a film set.

The 'hybrid' Being and film star lookalike, Janice, apprehensively pondered the unthinkable. 'Might I just be meeting my match?'

Spot thought, *I've seen it all now.*

Cat seized the situation, relieving her aunt of the awkward moment.

'Cameron! What brings you to the Queen of the South, and so far from your dream palace?'

'You know the answer to that question, Cat.'

She did, indeed. Cat, only wondered how Cameron and his mysterious wife had taken so long to find them. Aunt Therese, for once, seemed at a loss.

'We need to catch up, Cameron,' Cat said, glancing pointedly at her aunt. The yawn-faking Aunt Therese caught the hint.

'Well, dear, it's getting a bit late for long conversations, don't you think?' she said, looking up at the grandfather clock as it obligingly reached its eleventh chime. 'I think it's time for bed. Let's see if I've got room to put you all up!' Thinking, *we'll sort the nuts and bolts in the morning.* Aunt Therese was pragmatic if nothing else.

And with that, they all retired, Therese lapping up the excitement. In a brief space of time, Tara's and her dull existence had been transformed.

Cameron, somewhat deflated, sensed his entrance may have fallen short of the mark. His wife, after scanning the fresh territory and picking up signals, allowed herself a sense of gratification at meeting her potential saviour in the flesh.

Meanwhile, huddled together in Tara's basket next to the Aga, Spot asked, 'So, you and your owner crave a bit of excitement in your lives?'

'Yeah! So?'

'Well, be careful what you wish for.'

Chapter 28

The New Order

The less-than-inviting, poorly maintained establishment challenged the debutante to enter. The irritating, fine drizzle blew into her face as she climbed the death-defying slippery steps, negotiating the crucial missing bits.

The money on offer, initially, was nowhere near her hospital salary, which added to her feeling of *what the heck am I doing here?* She pressed the doorbell, anyway, her expectations as low as her mood.

The door flew open. An intensely good-looking African-Caribbean man exuded an unbridled welcome.

'You must be Emma. Our future star. I'm Tim. Come on in.'

Oh, my! Things are looking up, Emma thought, her negative perceptions rapidly replaced with, *well wow, maybe!*

'Tea, coffee; black, white?' The colossus asked as he led the way to his office.

Tim enthused positivity, reminding her of her 'all can do, and let's do it now' acquaintance, Roxy. He motioned the potential recruit to take a seat; and joined her. Another equally cheerful fella set two cups of coffee down on the table, as requested.

With no bidding from his boss, the overly forward guy introduced himself. 'Hi, Emma! I'm William, but please call me Wills.'

Emma smiled sweetly, thinking, *Crikey, what have I done to deserve this reception?*

Tim resumed, noting her demure demeanour while casting a discreet, disapproving glare at his colleague. Emma, not missing a trick, smiled to herself and sensed an opportunity to play one against the other to her advantage. An elated Tim couldn't wait to get things started.

'I've read your C.V., Emma. In it, you outline a story that you think might have legs. Would you like to elaborate?'

Emma cleared her throat.

'Well, without wishing to appear as a one-trick pony; the story is not only based locally but also features a person who, through no fault of his own, is a scapegoat for a terrible crime that shocked the community to the core. Perhaps you may have heard about it?'

'Err . . . you'd better jog my memory, Emma.'

Emma relayed the story, from the start to the present, while feeling nervous that she was in danger of overcooking the content. She finished, took a deep breath and looked up at her imposing potential boss, apprehensive that he might not be sharing her optimism.

'Relax, Emma!' Tim said, noting her endearing self-deprecation. He looked across quizzically at Wills, hoping he would return to a professional way of thinking. Emma looked at them both, acknowledging their genuine anticipation. Suddenly, everything was possible, the vibes reaching the roof. Massively relieved, she realised that her difficult, career-changing decision might well be the correct one.

Tim smiled broadly and, shaking her hand, said the words she had only dreamt about: 'Welcome to our innovative new publication, The New Order.'

Emma, well-read as she was, had often imagined that coveted cloud-nine moment. 'Well, baby,' she announced to herself, 'here it is!'

Wills loitered in the background, not wanting to intimidate this nervous-looking candidate any more than he may have done already. He had to admit an attraction to this promising raw talent. Momentarily, his thoughts turned to his complicated private life. He quickly reigned them in; 'Let's not go there. I need to move on.' Wills looked again at this uncut gem with a *je ne sais quoi* presence. Her immaculately attired body was slim, yet verging on the voluptuous. His inclination was to help her every step of the way. *What else could the self-proclaimed God's gift to women do?*

Emma, noticing that masculine take on her body, also noted she'd need to take nothing for granted. But the strong-of-character new recruit mischievously wondered what he might deliver in the future—personally and professionally.

'So, Emma,' Tim interjected, wary of his colleague's track record and quickly retaking control. 'we have an overflowing in-tray to clear, and we're rather short of genuine talent.' Tim couldn't resist another compliment and a slight dig at his present employee. 'So, bearing that in mind, Emma; when can you start?'

The analogy of the precarious entrance was not lost on the astute newbie. Emma, smiling to herself, now considered the dodgy steps she'd need to negotiate. Not least Will's potentially problematic attention. Nevertheless, she instantly came to her decision. 'Tomorrow?'

'Well, in that case, Emma, you are now officially on the books of the fastest-growing regional newspaper in the UK!'

Tim pronounced.

'Wow, thank you!'

Wills was also beside himself, optimistic that something might happen with the new girl in the future.

Interpreting his body language, Emma fixed him with an icy stare, thinking, *well, big guy, prove yourself, dick head and I might even think about it.*

Reading her, Wills wobbled, but only ever so slightly. *Demure? I'm not sure about that,* he mused.

Emma turned at the door, thanking Tim and Wills effusively for taking a chance on her.

'Not any sort of problem, Emma,' Tim replied, smiling. 'Look forward to seeing you tomorrow!'

She picked her way down the treacherous steps, thinking, *Okay, I might just have exaggerated the potential Wills problem,* when a song came into her head. *How appropriate,* she thought.

Emma skipped down the road, heading to her parked car. She had a new job. Her boss was cool, and there was the prospect of a 'challenging' love interest. She was now, *Dancing in the Street.*

Chapter 29

The Night Visitors

Cat, afforded the comfiest bed, courtesy of her doting Aunt, felt guilty, and lonely. She got up and quietly searched the upper landing for her enduring love. She was grateful that Aunt Therese had left a few night lamps on.

Low rhythmic snoring led her to a body tossing and turning, trying to find an ideal sleeping position on the sparsely padded, makeshift bed. Without success, it appeared.

Cat leant down and, peering through the gloom, instantly recognised Declan. She whispered in his ear. 'Hey, Lover.'

He opened his eyes. His tired brain was surprised by this unexpected intervention. Recognising the radiant face of his *raison d' être*, he hoped that heaven might just be here on earth.

'What is it, Cat?' Declan asked, suddenly feeling something major might be on the cards.

'Declan, I didn't realise you were sleeping rough. My Aunt won't mind, I'm sure.'

Declan, coming round, couldn't contain himself. 'Won't mind about what, Cat?'

'Well, the times, they are a-changing. Come on, I've got the best seat in the house, and I want to share it with you.'

After all the shit that he had endured, a still out-of-it Declan followed, with absolutely no carnal expectations—despite the—was it a hint from Cat?

Cat, at long last, felt now might be the time to re-evaluate their restrained relationship. Back in North Yorkshire, when Declan had given her a loving, welcome hug, everything else in the future was her vision. *Was that time now?* But then the vision of her heartthrob—Roxy—came into her mind.

Declan instantly took in this fabulous vibe, simply indulging in the huge heart of this incredible woman. His enduring sentiment.

'Cat, if you are happy, I am happy!'

Cat's love for this guy knew no bounds. One day, Cat speculated, 'The three of us will be together.' Declan indulged in that hug, probably not fully appreciating Cat's meaning.

Aunt Therese woke up, thinking she had heard something untoward. Her trusted senses, however, told her everything was okay. She smiled an overdue smile, coupled with a long, drawn-out sigh of contentment. Therese knew what might be 'going down' in the bedroom next door and she approved, of course.

But there was another noise. This time, outside. Therese rushed to the window to see headlights and a vehicle making its way from her house. She rushed downstairs and peered out of the lounge window. The light-coloured car was disappearing. Therese checked Anthony and Cleopatra's room. Empty. She decided she'd have to sort it out in the morning.

'Bejesus!' she muttered. 'Oim pretty knackered. It's the middle of the night.'

Looking to the end of her comfy bed, the wily woman of steely Irish descent noted the absence of her furry partner—she hadn't seen him since the 'invasion.'

'Sloopy, wherefore art thou?' a concerned Therese whispered. Not wanting to wake anyone up and noting the abandoned 'bed' on the landing, Therese tiptoed down to the kitchen to find her cat and provide him with some sustenance.

The cat, of course, had been majorly spooked by the unusual comings and goings and had retreated to a trusted safe haven, the garden shed. The nocturnal Sloopy noticed the light coming on in the kitchen. He knew it would be his loving owner. He shot across to the back door, scratching it for all his worth. Therese opened it gently.

'Gad bless ya, Sloopy! Come on in and have some grub. You must be famished.'

As Therese set the bowl down, the hungry cat meowed its thanks and tucked in. Back in her bed, Therese, before succumbing to a desperate period of recuperation after a day like no other, reflected on her choice of name for her wonderful feline friend. The infectious melody, 'Hang On Sloopy', performed in an understated fashion by the McCoys, had inspired her. The lyrics outlining a young woman's forthright attempts to rise above her situation resonated with her past life. That was a period in which she kept very much to herself, yet it had defined her destiny.

Therese decided she'd like to pick a moment to talk this through with her niece if ever the possibility arose. She had to ask herself, why was this all coming back to her now? Cat would provide the answers, she was sure of that. Fulfilled by the present exciting times and anticipating more, she reprised, 'Hang On Sloopy, Sloopy, Hang On'. Spot and Tara shot bolt upright in their communal bed.

Inside, the house was quiet. It was way before the humans would normally get up. The dogs' sensitive ears pricked up. Sounds were coming from outside. They scuttled into the front room and onto the sofa under the window, where they had a good view of the drive. There were three police cars parked on the far side of the road under the trees. Several figures were standing behind the cars, engaged in conversation.

'Keep quiet, Spot, and stay here. I'll get Therese,' Tara commanded.

As he reached the stairs, he met the ever-alert Therese coming down to investigate the noise she'd also heard. Tara and Therese joined Spot at the window.

'Right! This calls for action.' announced the resourceful lady of the house. 'Wait here guys.'

Spot nudged Tara. The Bedlington knew exactly what would follow, but Spot was somewhat bemused. Then it all became clear. The formidable Therese returned from her secret hideaway armed with her weapon of choice.

There was a thud-thud of footsteps on the stairs as the rest of the disturbed household appeared.

'Crikey Aunt! The cops are finally onto us,' yelled a rattled Cat.

Declan stood next to her, apprehension to the fore. 'Don't you worry none, Bab, Oile soon show 'em who's boss.' And with that, Therese unlocked the front door and strode out, her trusted shotgun held high, in a show of clear intent.

'What do you want, coppers?' she shouted in a voice that exuded threatening confidence.

An officer made his way from behind the cars, stopped in the middle of the road and called back, 'We have reason to believe a dangerous, convicted killer is being shielded at this property. Is this the case?'

Therese simply looked up, spotted a roosting magpie on a branch a few feet above the cop's head, took aim, and fired. Blood and feathers rained down. A direct hit on the unnerved cop, who rapidly returned to his defensive position with his equally dismayed colleagues.

'Jesus, detective!' a shaken constable called out. 'We need backup, and fast.

The PC, brushing the debris from his uniform, agreed. 'Get on the blower, now! Meanwhile, keep your heads down and I'll see if I can reason with her.'

The cops looked at each other, not confident about the outcome.

'Good luck with that, Sir!' one called back.

The PC advanced, but seeing the shotgun-toting woman retreating into the house, quickly thought better of it. 'Discretion is the better part of valour,' he murmured to himself. His colleagues merely smiled their knowing looks, noting that their newly promoted gaffer had a thing or two to learn yet.

'Crikey, Aunt! You had us going then,' Cat said.

'Ah Be-Jesus, Oie was just re-establishing the order of things hereabouts.'

'I guess they'll send for armed backup,' Declan suggested. 'That could take time. Are we stocked up on essentials, Aunt?'

'Don't worry about that, young fella. We can last for weeks. We've done it before, and we'll do it again!' Aunt Therese replied enigmatically.

The diminutive warrior double-checked her house, ensuring windows, doors and locks were secure.

'Now, while we have the chance, someone can help me fix us a decent bit of grub. We're going to be in for a long night.' Therese said, glancing across at her favourite niece, who took the hint and instantly followed Aunt T into the kitchen.

It sure was a long night. Janice and Roy managed to get a bit of sleep, but Therese, Declan, and Cat kept a constant vigil. Spot and Tara also did not stray far from the windows.

At the crack of dawn, a loud thudding shattered their peace. Two armed police officers were at the door.

One officer shouted through the letterbox, 'Mrs O'Leary, are you in there? This is the police. We have important information for you, which I'm sure you'll be interested in.'

An upstairs window above the front door opened silently. Aunt Therese poked her shotgun through the window and called out to her adversaries below.

'You must think I was born yesterday, coppers. Can't you take a hint? Get out of here.'

With that, she picked a spot across the road, again in the trees, and fired. The astounded cops bid a hasty retreat to join their colleagues behind the cars. It was the DI this time who took control of the unpredictable chaos, and Aunt Therese was anything but predictable.

The DI grabbed a loud hailer and, as calmly as he could, announced, 'Mrs O'Leary, we are here to tell you that the man we suspect you of harbouring, a Mr Declan Mitchell has been found not guilty of the double murder of the two schoolgirls. He is now considered a free man.'

'Don't give me that bollocks, you lying coppers!' Therese yelled from the window as she fired off another shot—this time lower.

'Holy shit! The woman's deranged. Let's back off for a while!' the DI exclaimed, scratching his head for inspiration.

In the house, Cat and Declan digested the unexpected statement from the cops. 'Crikey, Cat! He could be telling the truth,' Declan said.

'I'll get the laptop fired up,' Cat said. 'There should be a government website that will tell us of any developing court cases.' She felt a rush of blood, but inwardly cautioned herself. 'Bloody hell. Here it is, look!'

Declan swayed a touch, the gravity of the situation taking its toll after all this time. Therese appeared; fuming with rage. 'Those bastards won't get the better of Therese O'Leary. No way!'

'Aunt! Aunt!' implored Cat. 'Come and sit down with Declan and me. The article shows they really are telling the truth. They've pardoned Declan!'

'Ah computers, I don't trust them, never will!' Therese would need some persuading! Declan took over, 'Aunt, the details are all down here, there's no ambiguity, I'm free!'

'Oi don't know what your 'biggity' means, but are you both sure?' Therese was softening at last.

'Yes Aunt, but let's go over it again to be one hundred percent certain.'

'Okay, Gad bless ya, Bab.' A hundred per cent was more like her odds.

Therese afforded herself some overdue relaxation. 'Tara, wherefore art thou when Oi need ya the most?' Her dog, sensing relief at the unrelenting tension, nuzzled up to her. 'And here is our friend Spot! Oile make us all a noice cuppa.'

Cat and Declan just sat there, daring to imagine things were working out at last. Unlike Cat, Declan remained anxious. 'What about my next-door neighbours, Shannon and Ronan?' he asked himself. 'What about the other murders?'

Roy remained bemused, while Janice sat with an impartial look on her face, weighing up this latest development and the implications of her future plans. Outside, the cops were considering their next move. The DI, when asked, simply stated, 'Once bitten, twice shy. Give it time.'

The Being, possessing the spirit of the unassuming ex-nurse Janice, awakened. After a period of review and readjusting itself to the earthly body, it considered its options. Unlike her previous host, Kayleigh who came with significant 'baggage'. Janice, on the other hand, seemed relatively stable. But then, who knows what lurks beneath any surface? Whereas Kayleigh was definitively 'hands-on', Janice, the Being preferred others to do her dirty work for her.

Spot readjusted himself, knowing that his powers would shortly be required to prevent calamity.

'For fuck's sake,' Tara spat. 'Keep still. I need some sleep after all the stuff going on today.'

'Sorry, Scottie,' a concerned dog muttered ...

'And stop calling me Scottie. I'm a Bedlington Terrier in case you hadn't noticed, and my name is Tara.'

They drifted off, each to their own peace. Another day, another problem. Spot's addled mind went into dream mode.

> *'Bitch,' the dog spat out, not directed at his intended, but what was her name?*
>
> *'Yeah, got it, Joanne.'*
>
> *Trixie communicated with Spot. 'Listen to me. Six o'clock at the park?'*
>
> *Enjoying his Mc Doggy Delight, Spot picked up the ethereal message.*
>
> *'I thought I would never see you again. But yes, I can't wait. Where have you been? Have you had problems?'*
>
> *'Don't bloody ask. Ma 'owner', Joanne, hadn't got a clue how to empathise with a canine. I had to leave and fend for myself.'*
>
> *'So, you became a sort of feral being?'*
>
> *'Yeah.'*

Spot woke with a start—the dream still fresh in his mind. He looked around, trying to figure out where he was and what was happening to him.

Tara couldn't take any more. He slunk off to the lounge, cursing under his breath, 'Bloody Sassenachs!'

Spot, alone now, considered his position. Dreams were one thing, but the thought of Trixie, at some point, reappearing, nonetheless, instilled hope and expectation.

Chapter 30

Kids, Who'd Have 'Em?

'Jerome, Tyrone! Come down here, please,' Brenda called out.

The gaming kids, only too aware of their mum's incessant exhortations, albeit weary of another repeat, couldn't stop now. No way.

Brenda, anticipating this negative response, gave them a few reasonable nanoseconds to respond. Then, hearing nothing and feeling her blood boiling commanded, 'Get yourselves here. NOW.'

'Okay, okay! What's the big deal?' they muttered, reluctantly putting the game on hold.

The fourteen-year-old twins, wary of their mum's irritable temper, skulked down from their bedroom. Pointedly banging their feet down the bare wooden staircase, they shuffled into the compact kitchen below, smelling of burnt food, where they encountered a frazzled mother sitting at the tiny table.

'There is a story going around in these parts about a murder ... ' Brenda looked at her offspring, almost accusingly; the idea being to provoke a response.

'Yeah, what the fuck?' was the terse reply.

'Well, in your lingo, I think you and your pals might just be in a bit of shit,' Mum suggested, pushing the agenda ever so slightly.

The lads exchanged doubtful looks, speculating that their mum might have started on the white wine already. But then 4.30 pm was a bit early, even for her!

'Your tea will have to wait. I need to show you both something.'

Brenda brushed past them into the front room. Behind her back, Tyrone smiled to himself. *It ain't all bad then!* he thought, glancing across at his equally smirking brother.

Returning, and undeterred by this unhelpful vibe, Brenda set down a copy of the new local paper on the table, and invited her troublesome sons to take in the lead story, shouting out from the front page: 'Convicted Murderer Innocent?' Underneath, the report expanded the story, accompanied by a picture.

This man, Declan Mitchell, was found guilty of the horrific killing of two teenage school girls in Polesworth last year. Find out inside how a campaign is being waged to establish the truth and, against the odds, free an innocent man.

The boys froze, looking at each other again, this time not in their previous cocky fashion but with the grim realisation that something bad was in the air. And it wasn't only their mum's dodgy cooking!

'Sit yourselves down in the lounge.' Brenda felt a tiny glow, anticipating her plan might just bear fruit. 'I'll make us a drink and we can try to piece together what exactly happened on that fateful night.' She had to exude confidence to give herself a chance to make a difference: she knew that. *How am I doing?* She asked herself, feeling a tad more positive. *Keep it going.* A voice in her head answered.

Jerome was not convinced the outcome would be at all okay. He glanced across at his shell-shocked partner in crime. Tyrone's puzzled face betrayed similar feelings. But they sat down as instructed anyway—intrigued by what might follow.

Mum returned, equipped with her diminutive but hopefully effective armoury. The pop and junk food addicts, wouldn't normally drink 'boring' stuff like tea, but when offered it this time, they accepted gracefully. To their credit, they twigged straight away the gesture was less a drink and more a peace offering. A knowing look from Mum acknowledged the point. The boys, used to synthetic kicks, anticipated a changing landscape. For his part, Jerome caught his breath and glanced across at his brother, thinking, *we ain't gaming, this is for real.* Tyrone, forever the cynic, was visibly softening. Brenda, noting this reaction, sincerely hoped so. She appreciated that his uber-mistrustful smirk was gradually morphing into a more guarded smile.

The long overdue, reunited family group sat silently sipping their refreshments, apprehension at the fore. They swigged down the last drops.

'Right,' Mum began. 'You both asked me how I could possibly know about your involvement with the murdered schoolgirls . . . '

'We had nothing to do with the murders, Mum, for God's sake,' Tyrone cut in. 'I know we can be pains in the arse, but there's a limit!'

Jerome pitched in, backing his brother up in no uncertain terms. 'Come on . . . Mum?'

She jumped in, quickly trying to bring the situation back under control. 'No, no! I wasn't accusing you of anything.' *Christ,* she thought, knowing she had got off to a bad start. *This ain't going to be easy.*

The kids just sat there, confusion reigning; back to square one. Knowing her limitations and not being used to this kinda stuff, Brenda forced herself to summon up untapped powers, knowing she only had one chance.

'Look! Let me start again. Phew! Are you able to tell me what went down that night? Trust me, you will not be in trouble if you both tell the truth.'

'Yeah, but it's all right for you to say that,' Jerome said. 'What if we can't remember everything and somehow make things worse?'

'Okay, okay. I've got a better idea.' She went for it. 'Bearing in mind your concerns, how about if I tell you what I think may have happened? Please listen carefully. I'll try to get it right, but if I've got bits wrong, you will just have to stop me, and we'll talk.'

The bad boys sensed a more positive way forward. Resigning themselves to listen, they conceded this course of action might be the way out of this shit. So, with nothing to lose, they backed off.

'Go for it, Mum,' Tyrone said.

A relieved and semi-triumphant parent began her rendition. The boys, waiting with bated breath, could only guess at how much their mum knew or didn't know.

'On the way home from school one night, you two ended up on top of a bridge. You must have heard or seen something. Thinking something strange was about to happen, you got your phones out and started filming.

'The mist got worse, making it difficult to see clearly. There were terrible screams, and a figure appeared to shove two, what looked like schoolgirls covered in blood, into the canal. A lone man stood further back down the towpath looking on. You must have panicked or become incapacitated for whatever reason because the images shot around all over the place before you stopped recording.

'Your heads, maybe, had started turning upside down ...?' Again, another pause, looking for a reaction.

A nonplussed duo stared: no reaction.

Brenda carried on. 'I presume you turned tail and made for home, fearful that someone would find out what you had really been doing. You realised that you should have reported what you saw to the police, but that was a complete no-no, given the circumstances.'

Jerome and Tyrone, looking at each other for the nth time, could not believe how accurate their mum's imagined scenario was.

'But how did you know what was on our phones, mum?' Tyrone spurted out.

'Because, when you finally stumbled into the house; majorly worse for wear,' Mum emphasised, again looking for their reaction, 'one of you dropped your phone without realising—till the next morning when you had recovered from whatever you had been 'experimenting' with. I know your passwords: sorry. So I checked the contents and found the video, which, for some reason, was a bit trembly.'

The guilty pair, shoulders slumped, finally twigged that their mum had figured out they had been trying out dodgy, free drugs. To the novices' credit, they knew once they were hooked, they'd be included on the list of other losers contributing considerable sums of dosh to those big kids' lucrative side-line. Dealing in more addictive stuff. So it was always going to be a one-off for them.

'Look!' Mum continued, 'I'm not bothered about what you were taking because I presume you haven't done it since. Am I correct?'

'Yeah, of course,' Tyrone confessed. 'It was horrible. My head was all over the place. The last time I felt that bad was when we finished off that half bottle of whiskey last Christmas.'

Jerome nodded, smirking sardonically again. He had trouble quitting that habit. Brenda, feeling a long overdue connection with her offspring, sensed the mood lightening. *Thank God. Something good is coming out of this*, she thought.

'So now, the point is, you've done nothing that will get you into trouble. But what you have on your phones is evidence the police will be interested in.' Mum suddenly had a moment of panic. 'You still have the videos, don't you?'

On hearing the P word, the boys also panicked. But realising the importance Mum was giving to the situation, Jerome confirmed they still had the videos.

'Thank God for that! On top of this, they have convicted a possibly innocent man of the murder of these two girls. Even with the mist obscuring the identity, your evidence shows a slightly built woman carrying out the attack, with a random man standing well away from the scene. The man accused of the murder is nowhere to be seen.'

Brenda dared to think the tide may well be turning. The words directed at her now by an amenable and newly sympathetic son gave her renewed hope.

'So, what do you want us to do, Mum?' Jerome asked. 'I mean, reading that article shocked both of us. They sent that man to prison. He escaped, and he's now on the run for something he probably hasn't done.'

'We have to go to the police with this,' Mum confirmed.

'Let's go for it,' Tyson said. 'We might even become heroes.' Jerome was well up for it.

Tyson chipped in with, 'We might be in a situation like that one day and it'd be great to think someone might be there to help us out!'

Crikey, Brenda thought, *I never expected to hear big-hearted stuff like that coming from my kids!*

The reformed duo, for now at least, ran back up the stairs with renewed vigour, their jet-black tousled locks bobbing to and fro. As they sat back down to restart their game, they briefly reflected on their changed priorities in life. And decided it was time to resume their sodding game, anyway.

The out-of-necessity hard-case mum reflected on the day she'd just endured. She wished her husband could have been here to witness the potential redemption of their two, previously out of control, offspring.

It was suddenly all too much for an endlessly put-on mum. She settled onto her favourite chair; the indulgent tumbler of strong Jamaican rum tempered with orange caressing her lips, before she took that oh-so-wonderful first sip. Then, she thought, What the heck! We're all in this together now.

Thinking forward to the meeting with the police, she mentally implored her twins might take inspiration from M People's song lyrics: *'Search for the hero inside yourself, until you find the key to your life.'*

The boys suddenly became distracted from their intense game, thoughts simultaneously returning to the scary interrogation with the cops. As one, they pledged to search for their heroes within and take whatever shit might be thrown at them. Jerome and Tyson were well up for this now. And of course, their mum absolutely deserved nothing less.

Chapter 31

Emma

The New Order had sold out within hours of its release, requiring a new print run. Struggling to cope with the logistics as a result of the sensational response to the newly created format and hard-hitting main story. Tim afforded himself a period of reflection. He knew his carefully assembled team would rise to the challenge.

Congratulating himself as an excellent judge of character in hiring the *find,* Emma, he remained apprehensive about Wills and the effect he may have on her. He needn't have worried.

At first glance, demure Emma was anything but. She was adept at concealing these characteristics and found it faintly amusing to note the various reactions from her new acquaintances.

Tim's able back-up team was well-positioned to take on the extra workload generated; allowing the editor to resume his normal duties, one of which was his personal favourite: 'Letters to the Editor'. These otherwise innocuous rejoinders provided valuable feedback for an editor. In the days following publication, a plethora of offerings from *Joe Public* arrived in the post and via email, the majority inspired by the 'Innocent Man' story.

One of these, contributed by a Seán Black, took his eye. Seán had sent in a letter and optimistically included his ambitions to write a regular column for the paper.

He'd tentatively dreamt up a title, 'Seán and the Lad', a light-hearted take on a plumber and his young apprentice, and the shenanigans they got up to on their various jobs.

Seán's suggestion intrigued Tim. He envisaged it as a means of providing light relief from the more serious matters that concerned the paper's valued readership. The more he thought about this new concept, the more he liked it, pretty confident it had sure-fire potential.

Impulsively, the editor returned to his computer to take another look at Seán Black's email. He read it out loud to confirm to himself whether this latest wannabee's writing might have mileage.

Dear Editor, Please allow me to start by congratulating you all at The New Order for creating such a fresh and informative piece of journalism. In contrast to the repetitive rubbish trotted out by the established newspapers, and the TV, your content and innovative approach is a welcome breath of fresh air. Your team exhibits delightful talent, especially Emma Thompkins for her excellent coverage re. the 'Innocent Murderer'. Exceptional journalism.

The main point I would like to make is: I found myself in a similar situation to Declan, because the police considered me as a suspect for a murder that I obviously didn't commit.

To cut a long story short, I was cycling along a canal. My tyres went through a pool of blood, which later proved to be that of the victim. DNA checks found the splashes of blood on my bike matched the murdered woman. The police interrogated me intensely, and I became the prime suspect. It was only when the actual killer was located and convicted that I was released without charge. I made the point to my solicitor: in the absence of this fortunate-for-me outcome I would have been convicted and sent to prison. I asked him: 'How can our system be fair to allow that scenario?' He had no answer.

So, yes, I sympathise with the seemingly innocent man in his terrible situation and wish him all the best of luck; he's going to need it!

Seán Black via email. Address supplied. PostScript.

Dear Editor, I hope you decide my letter is worthy of publication. I am currently writing my memoirs and have ambitions to publish them. I am considering sending the opening story for your perusal. In the unlikely event that you approve, what would be the chances of this becoming the first instalment of a regular column in the New Order? If you don't ask, you don't get, after all! Seán Black.

The editor appreciated the letter was free of unnecessary waffle. He anticipated Mr Black's story might be of a similar ilk, and decided, there and then, to contact the author to encourage him to submit a trial edition of Seán and the Lad. He had a good feeling about it. This was the sort of material he knew the proles wanted to connect with.

Tim understood instinctively that Seán wanted to write for people who wouldn't normally read because they perceived the written word as boring and hard work. To crack that would open up a massive untapped market.

Tim totally bought into the angle that Seán was trying to access—they could have been brothers!

He looked forward to receiving the first edition.

When Seán received the reply, he just had to go for it. He picked out his—he thought—carefully written first part of his prospective memoirs. And selecting The New Order's email address, he pressed send.

To celebrate the success of the 'Innocent Man' story, the stars of the moment decided on a night out at the local, modest pub & curry house.

Wills, supercharged now, sensed an opportunity in his pursuit of the sensation that had shown up out of the blue. His confidence knew no bounds.

'What's your poison, my sweet?' he ventured, expecting a rum and coke at the high end of his 'intendeds' spectrum. And he was watching his pocket.

'Well, Big Boy, you and I have pulled off a result: getting onto the front page. Our supremo, Tim assumed it would happen, and now, guess what? He's ecstatic. And for that reason, a double Scotch, for starters, please.'

Emma's expectations of the romantic kind were next to zero, while in Wills' case, the opposite was true. It was early and the table near to the inviting log fire, the best in the house, was vacant.

They took off their coats, sat down and luxuriated in a simple pleasure.

'This is the life,' Emma purred.

Wills' attention, however, was temporarily drawn to a barmaid heading toward them, weighing up her next conquest.

Typical, thought his date, not missing a trick.

Meanwhile, the exhibitionist waitress wantonly displayed her 'goods' for the deliciously handsome punter in her line of fire. She took their order, weighing up her chances. Wills, not really getting it, simply went for the hottest curry, if nothing more, to prove a point. Emma chose a Korma.

'If that's everything, I'll be back shortly with your drinks,' the temptress breathed, shooting a glance at the dishy male.

On her return, the barmaid leant over the table putting the drinks down, deliberately revealing more of her silky smooth, enticing flesh.

'Enjoy!' she purred.

Wills acknowledged this brazen gesture, smiling back in a look that promised the recipient his undivided attention at some point. The barmaid retreated, smiling at Will's partner. She loved to tease.

'I think you're in there, Wills!' Emma outwardly chuckled, but inwardly muttered a bitchy observation to herself, 'Minx!'

'It certainly looks it, but you are the apple of my eye tonight, Emma.' *Full of shit or what?* Emma thought but merely smiled him her thanks.

The unlikely couple looked at each other. Emma secretly scheming. Wills in heaven. Emma stared into his grey eyes. The journalist only saw equilibrium. He wouldn't be any sort of problem in her quest. She was pretty sure about that. Pleased with how things were going, personally and in her new career, she suddenly felt a desire to look further into the future.

'Time for a top-up?' a frothing Wills enquired, interrupting her thoughts.

Go for it, knobhead, Emma thought, but demurely replied, 'Yes please, Wills!'

Feeling replete, Emma considered her next step. She gave Wills a restrained peck on the cheek to keep him going. Wills almost wetting himself.

Emma figured it would be a good idea to give him a tad more rope with which to hang himself. But, considering the mess he was in, she realised that could wait. He was practically beyond the pale. The job was almost done.

'What d'you fancy my darling, apart from tarts like me?' she asked.

'Well, your place or mine?'

Emma took him to her place. It didn't look good. But her thoughts were elsewhere. It wasn't long before she had to shepherd her pathetic, inebriated 'lover' to her car, drive him home, and dump him unceremoniously onto his bed.

'Sorry, Wills.'

'Sorry Emma,' Wills just about managed to reply.

Back in the place that Emma called home: *What a day,* she thought, still relatively sober. She could take her drink. She poured herself another modest one, reflecting on her professional and personal efforts to date. *So far, so good.*

Tim, busy as he always was, found the time to check his inbox. There it was: the promised email with the first instalment from the prospective new columnist. He shut his door in a gesture that said to his guys, *do not disturb.* Sitting down, feeling hopeful, he began to read.

There was a caveat sitting in the back of his mind. However, he was content to put it to one side for now. *Bring it on, Seán the plumber. Impress me.*

Tim looked up from the screen. 'Wow, this prole may have some sort of connection. I think this column could have legs.' He vowed to call the author. The New Order, his pet project, needed continual input, and this was dynamite.

The all-powerful editor reflected on the motivation behind the plumber's need to change career direction. It struck a chord with his own situation. Both he and Seán were opening doors and making their way to their new reality.

If Seán could have been there to comfort his collaborator, he would have wished him all the best. Escapism can take over, of this, any creative writer is aware. On an impulse, Tim opened Seán's email and read it again to search for any more clues. There was a knock at his door.

'Enter.' The new kid on the block sidled in.

'Emma!'

'Sorry to disturb you, Tim, but I just wanted to thank you for everything.'

'Well, thank you, young lady. You've certainly landed on your feet here.' The editor felt absolution may be imminent. He wasn't sure why.

'Forgive me if I am speaking out of turn, but you seem to have been a bit apprehensive, recently, and speaking from experience, I recognise the symptoms.' Tim, taken aback, peered at this sensation and dared to wonder if this could be the answer to his seemingly interminable problems.

‘Please, sit down, Emma. I’ll get us coffees.’ Tim’s head was still swimming.

Emma conceded her goal was unlimited ambition. But she felt compassion for this guy. He needed help, and she would provide it. She sensed a win-win situation.

Chapter 32

Brenda

Mum wasn't timing it, but she guessed she'd been waiting to talk to someone for at least fifteen minutes. And she dared not put the phone down and start again, or she would have to repeat the more than laboricus process.

'Hello, West Midlands Police. How can I help?' At last, someone answered, albeit entirely disinterestedly.

'Oh, hello! My name is Mrs Brenda Jackson, and I have some information regarding a previous crime that I'm certain the police will be interested in.'

Brenda felt this might just be sufficient to garner the youngish-sounding officer's attention! She was not wrong.

PC Younger, sensing a promotion opportunity, quickly began the process. 'Certainly Madam. If you could elaborate, I'll see what I can do.'

The twins' mum briefly relayed the story, including dates, locations and names of the persons involved. The keen officer acknowledged this information and informed her he would contact his superiors and get back to her.

'You will get back to me, won't you?' a cynical Brenda asked.

PC Younger replied in the affirmative.

Brenda put the kettle on, not holding her breath. But then, she thought, The New Order had made a big impact with its exposé of a miscarriage of justice. And the authorities can get the jitters over this sort of thing. She knew that from experience.

The kids arrived home from school early, for once.

'Hey, Mum, how did it go!?' Tyrone asked, his enthusiasm through the roof.

'Yeah, I got through. They're going to get back to me.' The inevitable, uber-cynical twins' looks said it all. But just as they were about to trudge up to their room, disappointed, Mum's phone rang. The three of them stopped in their tracks.

'Go on, Mum, answer it! Put it on speaker.' Tyrone implored.

'Hello! Is that Mrs Brenda Jackson?' a polite voice enquired.

'Speaking.'

'Hello, Mrs Jackson, this is PC Younger of West Midlands Police. Regarding your new information about the crime in Polesworth last year, the investigating officers would like to visit you and your family at your earliest convenience.'

'Why, of course. Thank you, constable. Please hold the line.' Thinking on her feet, she mouthed, 'Saturday' at Tyrone and Jerome.

'Is Saturday morning okay?' Brenda asked PC Younger, noting the kids' furious nods.

'Of course, Mrs Jackson. Shall we say 10.30?'

'Perfect. We'll look forward to seeing you, then.'

'Detective Sergeant Agar and Police Constable O'Brien will be calling.'

'Okay, thanks for that.'

Brenda put the phone down, and organised as she was, copied the information onto her notepad. She knew she'd have to reassure the apprehensive twins. But before she did that, she had to point out some inevitable home truths.

'The chances are that these guys will want to know what you were doing on the bridge and why you didn't report it to the police. So we need to be ready for that.'

Tyrone said, 'Crikey, Mum. We can't tell them we were trying drugs, can we?'

She had to spell out this uncomfortable reality. 'I'm afraid we'll all have to be totally honest with them. These pros can spot an untruth a mile away. It's what they're trained to do.'

'But what if they arrest us and send us to prison?' Jerome yelled.

Mum dived back in. 'I'm sure it won't come to that. The police will just want to establish the truth regarding the murders. Trust me.'

Their doubts subsided, and the swagger returned. 'Well, I'm looking forward to it,' Tyrone said. 'Come on bro,' let's finish our game and we can go for the real stuff on Saturday.'

Jerome followed his brother upstairs, much to Brenda's relief who, if she cared to admit it, was not feeling as confident as she had appeared to her sons.

Out of her window, Brenda saw a car pull up a discreet distance away. It was of a nondescript appearance, thankfully. She hadn't wanted the neighbours speculating what a marked police car was doing at her house.

'Yes, come in!' Brenda responded to Detective Sergeant Agar's introduction of himself and Police Constable O'Brien.

She led them into the lounge and offered them a seat.

The twins appeared at the living room doorway, fidgeting their weight from foot to foot.

'And you must be Tyrone and Jerome?' WPC O'Brien ventured, looking up. Mum smiled at her lads, gesturing that they should relax and sit down. They got the message.

'Tea, coffee, anyone?' Brenda asked. She put the kettle on and returned straight away while it boiled. She didn't want the lads left alone with the cops; at least not yet.

Detective Sergeant Agar began, 'Are you aware of the facts of this case that occurred a year or so ago?'

They nodded.

The DS, turning to Brenda, carried on, 'Mrs Jackson, you reported to our PC Younger that you possess mobile phone footage of the scene of the crime at the canal. If this is correct, can we see it, please?'

Brenda got up. 'As soon as I learned of the importance of this footage, I confiscated the two phones and locked them away. I'll just fetch them.'

As the coppers viewed the footage, the unfolding events of the incident became clear. The mist made it difficult to make out the facial features of the assailant, but the body appeared to be that of a woman. The only other person, at a distance from the scene, was a lone man.

'Okay, we need to take these away to verify their authenticity and for forensics to check them out,' DS Agar explained. 'Now, can we all take a walk to the crime scene? I understand it's not far away, and the rain seems to be holding off.'

At the infamous Bridge 50, the small party attempted to imagine the terrible events that had taken place that night. The two wily cops observed the reactions of not only the boys but also their mum, searching for any hint that might contribute to a better understanding of what happened there.

'We've seen enough for now. Let's get you back home. It looks like it's coming on for rain.' PC O'Brien said, leading the way, as the flecks of drizzle dropped from the skies.

They took off their wet coats, and at Brenda's request, settled down in the lounge in front of a welcoming fire. The DS began. After a pause, he pointed out that he needed to ask a couple of important questions of Tyrone and Jerome. The lads, horror-struck, knew what was coming. They looked across at Mum.

'I think you both know what I am going to ask,' DS Agar said, 'so please don't get upset. Now, why were you on the bridge at that time of night and why didn't you report what you saw to the police?'

The lads had rehearsed their reply many times over. They agreed Tyrone would take the reins.

'Look mister, sir,' Tyrone said. 'We don't do drugs. No way, but some of the bigger kids at school talked us into trying out some of their stuff for free. I think they wanted to get us hooked, like all the others. We were on the bridge. It was awful. We both started puking up all over the place. We heard screams and got the phones out to film as best we could and then scarpered. How could we tell anyone? We'd get into serious trouble.' Tyrone broke off, tears filling his eyes.

WPC O'Brien came to his rescue. 'Look, it's okay, we understand. We're not here to trap you. We just want to establish who carried out the murder.'

The DS had the last question. 'Did either of you see who carried out the attack?' They couldn't remember.

'Alright, that's all for now,' the DS said as he and WPC O'Brien got up.

In the hallway, the two detectives thanked the Jacksons for their cooperation and informed them they would be in touch.

'If we consider there's sufficient new information to re-open the case, then we can go from there. Either way, we'll be in touch,' DS Agar said, as they all shook hands.

'There!' a relieved Mum said, as the door shut behind them. 'That wasn't so bad, was it?'

Tyson and Jerome simply sank back into the sofa. 'No,' they said in harmony.

'Right!' she announced. 'I need to get in touch with someone at The New Order Newspaper. I'm sure they will be very interested in our evidence.'

'Crikey, Mum, we don't want to jump the gun and upset the police, do we?' Tyrone spluttered.

'Well, son, nice enough as those guys were, the system might cause them to drag their feet a bit. I don't care whether I'm doing the right thing or not, but I'm determined to get the ball rolling—don't forget the innocent man on the run.'

'Let's do it, Mum. And maybe there'll be something in it for us.'

'Hello, The New Order. How can I help?'

Brenda briefly explained the situation and was told someone would call her back very shortly. The ever-cynical Brenda had heard it all before, of course, and with an exaggerated sigh thanked the otherwise helpful member of staff. Before she could get to the kettle, the phone in her pocket rang. It was the newspaper.

'Hello, Mrs Jackson? This is Emma from The New Order. I understand you have some crucial evidence concerning the miscarriage of justice story we ran last week.'

Brenda outlined what had occurred with the police and asked the young lady if the paper would be interested.

'We certainly would, Mrs Jackson. When would be a convenient time to call?' Emma was sensing blood.

'Well, the kids are back at school on Monday . . . '

Emma jumped in, 'My colleague and I can call round tomorrow.'

'Wow, on a Sunday? Are you sure?' 'Sure. About 11.30?'

'Great! I'll make sure the kids are up.' Brenda had a good feeling about this.

Chapter 33

In the News

Brenda felt in her pocket, fished out her phone, tapped a few keys and saw the image of the reporters waiting patiently at the front door looking quizzically at the camera doorbell, wondering if it worked.

She opened the door—'Emma?'—and ushered the intrepid reporters in to join Tyrone and Jerome in the lounge. Brenda offered them drinks, and when they were all settled, spelt out the state of play so far.

'We've had a very . . . err . . . pleasant visit from the police. They took all the relevant details. We went with them to the crime scene at the bridge on the canal. They say they'll decide whether to reopen the case soon. So I guess we'd better wait on that verdict. I mean, before the New Order makes the evidence public. Are you happy with that?'

Emma and Wills took it all in. Then, flashing a look at him and getting an affirmative vibe, he nodded his approval.

'Of course. We don't want to jump the gun and ruin everything.' Emma said. 'But, talking to our boss, he said instances such as this can escalate, become very high profile, and capture the imagination of an attentive public. And if that happens, the police are more likely to bow to public pressure to be seen trying to get to the truth, with no hint of a coverup.'

Brenda cottoned on quickly. 'So, what you are saying is; you can get the ball rolling without jeopardising our position?'

'Exactly,' Emma said.

Wills joined in, 'And before we set any copy up for final printing, we'll run it by you all to be sure you are happy with the content.'

Brenda and the twins voiced their approval, confident that this great new publication would deliver. Emma and Wills said their goodbyes and left.

'I'll give the cops another couple of days and then I'll chase it up,' Mum announced.

Tyrone and Jerome agreed. They loved it when she was in this positive mood and knew there would be more of it to come.

Tuesday arrived—09. 30 am—no contact from the police. Brenda rang WPC O'Brien's contact number. She said that number would get her through to them easier than the nightmare main number that took forever.

Someone answered within seconds, and Brenda asked if she could speak to WPC O'Brien or DS Agar. The officer asked what it was in connection with. Brenda explained. After a brief on-hold, the officer told Brenda that they were both unavailable and that one of them would call her back as soon as possible.

Brenda's mistrust kicked in again, but she simply replied, 'Okay, then. Thank you for your help, but please don't let me down. This is very important.'

'I understand, Madam,' came the standard reply.

By 11.00 am, Brenda had the washing machine on. The fifteen-year-old vintage model made such a racket that she didn't immediately hear her phone ringing on the windowsill.

As she grabbed her mug next to it she could see the screen flashing, showing an incoming call. In the nick of time, before it went to voicemail, she answered it.

'Mrs Brenda Jackson, please?' A voice asked. 'Speaking,' Brenda replied, instantly recognising the voice.

'Hello, Mrs Jackson, this is DS Agar from West Midlands Police. I have some good news for you.'

An ecstatic Brenda listened carefully. It seemed Emma and Wills had been bang-on regarding the police being extremely wary of alienating the public unnecessarily. They'd reopened the case.

'We'll be in touch regarding the details shortly, so please bear with us for a couple of days,' DS Agar added.

Brenda agreed, thanked him profusely, and put the phone down. And picked it straight back up to text her sons at school, noting it was near their lunch break.

Hey, T&J, did you get the message from me?

Right on! The twins texted back.

The twins high-fived each other. Things were looking up.

The fourteen-year-olds, with Mum in attendance, sat in silence as the kindly WPC read them their rights. The interview room at the police station afforded an intimidating atmosphere for the young lads, but they reminded themselves of their mum's earlier reassurance and took comfort from that.

DS Agar reviewed the evidence provided by Tyrone and Jerome and asked if they would like to add anything further. The reply was in the negative. As they left the DS informed them that his team would proceed with the investigations. Brenda thanked the detectives for their sympathetic diplomacy towards her and her sons. DS Agar noted this nuclear family, although missing a glaring member, possessed integrity. He considered they were worthy of his newly adopted policy to make PR an important consideration.

Brenda and the Twins

> *Convicted man in the 'Bodies in the Canal' murders pardoned by police.*
>
> *Following a concerted campaign by this newspaper and the ensuing public outcry, the police have reopened the case. They have gathered fresh evidence and concluded that the conviction of Mr Declan Mitchell is unsafe. He is now considered a free man. (More inside).*

Brenda gasped. She grabbed the latest edition of the New Order from the shelf and avidly scrutinised the article. They'd passed the copy to her the day before, but seeing it in print was a different ball game. She made a mental note to read the paper from cover to cover when she got back home from the convenience store.

'My kids,' she marvelled, 'making front page news!'

At this, she briefly reflected on her lonely life without her estranged husband. *How proud Tim would be,* she thought.

Back in her favourite lounge seat, Brenda tucked into her cheese and tomato sandwich, while her thoughts drifted again to her domestic situation. She tidied up, grabbed the New Order, and indulged herself with the lead story.

As intended, she delved deeper into the paper before halting at a promising article accredited to the Editor. She remarked to herself how well-written and easy to read it was. It reminded her of someone.

Pondering on who this editor might be, Brenda flicked through the small-print credits tucked in a corner. And there it was—the writer's name—Timothy R. Jackson.

Brenda sat stunned as she absorbed the implications. She looked at the prose again, not believing her eyes, but yes, it was there in black and white. Her husband had landed a plum job. Brenda had to concede that his journalistic talent was undeniable. She'd always felt proud of his achievements.

As it sank in, she tried to imagine her husband's reaction to learning of their sons' exploits and subsequent outings as heroes. Outings, which he, with the help of his wonderful staff, had initiated. More refreshments were called for. Coffee in hand, she sat down again, rerunning the past, the unexpected revelation still unnerving her.

The reality that they had not got on was an understatement. Her workaholic husband was perennially absent, and her explosive temperament didn't help. So, on a rare occasion when they were together, they decided it would be better for the sake of their kids that they should separate. That was two and a half years ago.

Brenda had quietly struggled since then and gradually yearned for a return to proper family life.

The hot-headed Brenda made the decision that she'd get in touch with the bloody editor. I owe it to myself and the kids.

At the appointed time, Tim pulled up outside the marital home, unsure if this was a wise decision.

The front door opened and there stood his wife. He got out of the car thinking, It's now or never. There was no embrace, Brenda simply ushered him in.

'Take a seat, Tim, while I make us a drink. Is it still black coffee, no sugar?'

He smiled an awkward acknowledgement.

The culinary sounds coming from the kitchen served as a poignant reminder of the simple things that he'd taken for granted. And looking at the paraphernalia lying around, of course, the massive things—his two wonderful kids he'd unbearably missed. Hurriedly, he wiped the unexpected tears from his eyes before his wife returned with their coffees.

Brenda looked searchingly into her husband's eyes and instantly realised her intentions were still valid. Tim reciprocated with a knowing look. They sat silently, wondering who should make the next move.

'Look, Brenda—'

'Tim, please,' they spluttered in unison—the absurd situation easing the tension, resulting in a laugh-out-loud moment.

The floodgates opened. They began discussing the past, present and possible future. Tim explained how he had helped to set up the New Order and the subsequent masterstroke in hiring the superstar. He considered using this as an excuse for his perceived indifference to his family values. He needn't have worried.

'Oh, you mean Emma Thomkins?' Brenda interjected. 'What a talent! What a paper ... and what an editor!'

They fell into another silence, both feeling a path was opening up which had a feeling of long overdue inevitability.

As the conversation ebbed, they each silently acknowledged the gains they had made. Tim looked across at his wife and knew it was enough for now.

'Look, Brenda, thank you so much for this. I have to go now. I'm sure we both need to take stock.' Tim got up.

'Oh, yes, Tim, absolutely. But please, call me when you're ready, and perhaps we can sit down again and decide where we are going?' Brenda said, getting a tad emotional.

Tim made a diplomatic exit after a very light embrace, confirming a resolution to their ongoing situation could be, at the very least, a possibility.

As he headed back to his deserted flat, he attempted to digest what had just occurred. It felt surprisingly positive. There was no current significant other. He was simply married to the job. Now, though, he hoped for a resolution to his wish to move on. But he reminded himself of the need for extreme caution. He also reminded himself that one reason for the marital split was his over-reaction to Brenda's extreme temperament, and her tendency to blow up at the drop of a hat.

He allowed himself a wry smile. That's what made it so unpredictable and hardly boring. He had to be realistic. Deep down, he knew he would have to come to terms with these truths, once and for all if they got back together.

Brenda stared out of the window as her husband disappeared out of sight. She allowed herself a moment of optimism. She recognised her own failings and sensed Tim probably did, too. Both of them would need to compromise, that was clear. The back door crashed open, and two tousled-haired teenagers stood in the doorway.

'Everything okay, Mum?' Jerome said, noticing a slight redness in his mum's eyes.

'Everything is fine, Jerome.'

'Good, what's for tea then, Mum? We're starving!' Tyrone added, speaking for his twin.

Brenda momentarily glimpsed the past, but now envisaged only a much better future. She breathed a sigh of relief.

'I'll see what I can find.'

The twins sat at the kitchen table eating the mushroom omelette, conjured up by the reborn chef.

'Wow, Mum, that was terrific,' Tyrone said.

Brenda smiled back, thinking now might be the time to tell the twins of her intentions. She cleared her throat. 'Listen up, boys. I have some further news.'

The boys sat forward on their chairs, all ears.

'Okay, Mum. What is it? Are we going to receive medals?' Tyrone joked optimistically.

'No, no, nothing like that, although you probably deserve them.' Brenda paused for effect. 'Your dad is coming back to live with us. Now I know what you are thinking—it will be all rows and fighting like it was before. But, I can assure you that will not be the case. We've talked this through, and we are both determined to make it work.'

The twins were gobsmacked.

'So, how do you both feel about it?'

'Wow!' they finally yelled in unison.

‘We’re gonna be together again!’ Jerome exclaimed.

‘Seriously?’ Tyrone queried.

‘Yes,’ Mum replied. ‘We are.’

Emma and Wills

Fresh from their recent triumph, Wills and Emma were in the pub in front of the roaring fire after a rewarding day at the New Order.

They had been in the field monitoring a rapidly growing protest movement. The government had finally sanctioned a highly controversial rail link which was to devastate large parts of the Midlands. The consensus was that it was;

a) ill-conceived,

b) environmentally disastrous,

c) a waste of money the government didn’t have, and

d) of extremely dubious benefit.

They debated their storyline.

‘I think this protest could snowball,’ Wills remarked. ‘It could go either way, I guess. But the bottom line is there will be plenty of fodder for us to exploit.’

Emma was quickly getting the hang of this job. And Wills would surely follow her lead. He wasn’t gonna give up on his target, Emma, anytime soon. That was for sure.

Cat

Cat decided it was time for action. Her doting aunt had finally accepted the cops were telling the truth. She got up and headed for the front door.

'Whatever are you doing, Bab?' Aunt Therese spluttered.

'I need to talk to these guys and see if we can defuse the situation,' Cat asserted.

Therese reached for her trusty weapon.

'Please, Aunt, you must put that out of sight, or we could all be back to square one.'

'Go on then, but oil be watching to make sure there's no monkey business. Gad bless ya, Bab!'

Roy jumped up. 'I'll come with you, Cat.'

'Thanks, Roy, but I think just one of us should go. We don't want to intimidate them.' Cat opened the front door.

'Boss,' an attentive cop called quietly. 'someone's coming out.'

Cat looked left, right, left. There was no traffic, as usual. She reached the centre of the narrow road and waited, trying to look as innocent and demure as she felt.

The senior cop slunk over. This lady didn't appear to be a threat, at least. Cat wasted no time on formalities.

'Officer, please allow me to apologise for my aunt's behaviour. She lives alone and is fiercely protective of what little she has.'

The cop immediately bought into Cat's convincing explanation. 'You're not wrong, young lady. Goodness, with her level of skill, we could sign your aunt up as a marksperson. Now I take it the ex-fugitive, Mr Declan Mitchell, is also living at this address. Is that correct?' he continued, feeling he was taking control of the situation at last.

Cat nodded, sensing this cop deserved the time of day at least. The previous tense atmosphere evaporated as Cat and the cop bonded.

'I'll go back, and I'll see if my aunt will let us in. Then you can see for yourself that she really is no threat at all.' Cat disappeared behind the front door, returning a few seconds later.

'Please follow me, Officer.'

The cop sat down a discreet distance from Aunt Therese, who, initially, made no pretence of accepting a hated copper on her territory.

'Janice dear, go with Roy and make us all a cup of tea.'

Therese congratulated herself on this one concession. The cop smiled, sensing an opportunity to steal Cat's limelight in the eyes of his demanding superior.

The tension eased, palpably. Cat felt relieved as she looked across at an increasingly relaxed Declan.

Janice and Roy returned, armed with the peace offering. They all accepted gratefully.

For her part, Cat became very aware of the need to get back to the Midlands. Declan was now a free man—mission accomplished. At least for now, was the caveat lurking in the back of her mind.

Swigging the last drop of tea, Cat sidled over to her heroic Aunt.

'We are going to pack our things tonight, Aunt and make an early start in the morning to get back home.'

'Oi understand, Gad bless ya, Bab!'

Therese waved her houseful of visitors off, holding Sloopy in her arms, Tara at her heels—her teary eye tempering the wily woman's mood.

'Come back up, any time you like, you'll be most welcome. Gad bless y'all.'

She watched them disappear, feeling only gratitude that she had been able to help her special niece and her friends.

'Come on, Sloopy. It's just you, me and Tara—for now!'

For Roy, as much as he had revelled in this recent escapade, the sight of his homecoming into view was comforting. The wintry hills they'd left behind were now largely snow-free and afforded the heavily laden Land Rover easy access to his property.

The next morning, Cat and Declan thanked Roy profusely for his support and hospitality. Janice was conflicted about Roy's offer—Should she stay or should she go? But with the Being inside her momentarily taking charge, she opted to return with Cat to the Midlands. She'd try to resume nursing back at the hospital—if they'd have her. A chilling smile crept across the Being's face as she reaffirmed her determination that Declan would never get away that easily.

Cat expressed similar job intentions. She was confident that Dr Hussain would support her: unless he'd been implicated as an accessory in Declan's escape. Declan and Janice would stay with Cat for now. For Janice, it would be only temporary until she could find her own digs. Cat's flat would be heaving, *but what other choice did they have?*

The arrangements unnerved Spot.

Despite the near miss at Aunt Therese's, the relationship between Cat and Declan continued its platonic trajectory. Cat reflected on the emotional mileage she had invested in looking out for this guy, and for the first time, asked herself a simple question—*why?* It was obvious to her that he was a normal person, massively wronged. Surely it was only natural for an angel like herself to fly to the rescue. Despite these new doubts, the ravages of the long campaign took its toll. Succumbing, Cat fell into a restless sleep.

In her dreams, Cat thought of her lover, Roxy, in mortal danger. Kayleigh had tried to take her. Declan lay in his bed, smiling and commanding the nurse before him to help him. She had no choice.

Cat awoke with a severe jolt. 'Roxy, I need you now!' She phoned and waited, and waited.

'Cat? Is that really you?'

'Of course, my love. Where are you?'

Roxy told her. She went.

Spot curled up in his basket under the kitchen table. A lot of water had passed under the bridge since he last slept there. His mind continually wandered back to the enigma that was Declan. And then to the extraordinary lengths to which Declan's acquaintances had gone to help him.

The police had convicted Kayleigh of four murders and one attempted murder. Spot thought back to the 'Bodies in the Canal' scenario. He tried to remember the events leading up to the fatal stabbings. Ronan had gone behind the towpath hedge to relieve himself. Declan called out to Ronan not to be surprised when he returned as the mysterious, charming, beautiful woman—Kayleigh. It would fly in the face of perceived wisdom, *but could Kayleigh have possessed Declan?*

The black-spotted Jack Russell gradually dozed off, massive doubts occupying his canine mind.

THE END

About The Author

Rob AKA Andrew R Bedlington, is based in the West Midlands, UK. Over the years, he has published numerous articles in local newspapers and professional journals.

His experiences as a plumber have afforded him many opportunities to meet and observe colourful life situations. Now semi-retired, he finally has the freedom to spread his writing wings and weave these life experiences into his thrilling stories.